Book May Be Kept

ABOVE GROUND LEVEL

ABOVE GROUND LEVEL

•

Theresa Goldstrand

AVALON BOOKS
NEW YORK

PRINTED IN THE UNITED STATES OF AMERICA
ON ACID-FREE PAPER
BY HADDON CRAFTSMEN, BLOOMSBURG, PENNSYLVANIA

To my mother, Irene, my "angel" whose patience, love, encouragement and support have given me the courage to fly. You are truly the "wind beneath my wings."

In appreciation for individual assistance and technical expertise without which this book would have been hopelessly flawed, I wish to thank Lem Dotson, Rob Gamble and Betty Gamble.

Chapter One

"Westair 143, this is Denver Center, do you copy?" The large PVD monitor cast a greenish pall on Angela Lawrey's face. Adjusting her headset, she waited for the pilot's response.

"Sure do, ma'am."

"Descend to two-zero-zero and take a niner-five heading south."

"Will do. Roger."

A lazy Southern drawl preceded the low chuckle that Angela had heard several times at this same hour of the day. She checked her watch and noted the time. *Four o'clock, one forty three is right on time.* She wondered about the man with the down-home drawl that sounded like he'd written the book on Southern charm. He seemed all too sure of himself.

Her gaze remained fixed on the intermittent slashes that rearranged themselves as the aircraft moved toward the busy landing pattern of Denver International Airport. She studied the moving targets with the intensity of a silent cat observing its prey. Angela scanned the perimeter for outlying aircraft that were due to arrive within a minute or two behind Flight 143.

Suddenly a skittering speck turned off its safe course and veered directly into the path of the giant commercial airliner.

"Westair 143. Previous issue traffic now turning northbound. Twelve o'clock. Two miles."

"I don't see traffic," the captain replied. "Request vector around it."

"Vector's impractical. Climb to flight level two-eight-zero. Over."

"Roger."

She prayed the jumbo jet could respond in time. Anxious seconds ticked by. The tiny blip continued to ascend while Westair Flight 143 angled sharply upward to avoid a midair collision. Unconsciously, she reached over and clutched the arm of her partner, Richie Lange. Richie scanned her screen, and together they studied the movement of the two moving specks. The seconds stretched into infinity, and she felt the muscles in her face tighten while waiting for danger to pass. The small target disappeared. Angela willed it to reappear beyond the path of the large plane. And then it happened. Westair passed over the top of the private craft.

"Whewee, baby." The captain of Flight 143 whistled over his radio. "That was a close one."

Hearing the nervous chuckling of the captain in her headset helped release the knot in her stomach. They had made it.

"Westair 143, Denver Center, are you all right?"

"I'm sure the passengers didn't mind that little bit of

rockin' and rollin'. It'll give them something to talk about when we land."

Sighing heavily, Angela squeezed Richie's hand and shook her head. "Descend to flight level one-eight-zero with a heading of two-five-zero. Reduce speed to two-five-zero knots then begin descent at niner five."

"Roger, Denver. What's your handle?"

Angela smiled, knowing personal conversation on the airways was strictly taboo. Maintaining the same even tone she had used when averting the potential disaster she replied, "AG. Over."

"Well, *AN-GEL*, I owe you a dinner and a humongous thank you. You'll be hearin' from me. One-four-three. Over."

Before she could take time for a much-needed break, Angela again focused on the PVD screen, directing two more jumbo carriers into the airport perimeter.

After she signed off, Angela released the breath she was holding in an audible "Whoosh."

Richie squeezed Angela's shoulder. "That was close!" she said, patting his comforting hand.

"You handled it just fine."

"It helped knowing you were here. It would've been my word against the world if they had collided."

"True." Richie nodded.

"I hate to think—"

"Don't. One less worry. It worked out."

"But what if that abort hadn't worked?" Angela shuddered.

"Point is, it did."

"Thank goodness that Westair pilot knew how to take orders."

"I'm surprised he reacted so quickly. He's good."

Angela smiled. *Whoever he is, he is good.* "I've had men on the line who'd argue with me over a directive like that. Challenge me."

"Because you're a controller, or a female?"

"Sometimes I think it's the latter. What about you?"

"Usually they just do what I say. I can't say they've ever argued with me thinking I was a female."

Angela shot him a disparaging look.

Richie threw his hands up in mock defense. "Just kidding."

"You're an incorrigible redhead, Richie. I bet you used to throw spiders at girls when you were little, didn't you?"

"Every chance I got."

"Shoot spitballs through a straw?"

"That too," he admitted.

"Your mother had her hands full."

"Yup."

"Break time, Lawrey."

Angela looked over her shoulder at the radar controller. "Sounds good to me. I'll be back in a few."

"Take your time."

"See you later, Richie."

Angela left the darkened control room for the ladies lounge. She thrust her hands under the cool water of the tap and let it run for a moment. Raising her head to scan her reflection in the mirror, she looked for the signs. She angled her head slightly to the left and noted the lines around her green eyes. Fatigue, stress, worry, tension— they had each added a line or two. "You're getting old, kid."

It was nearing the end of her shift. Another two hours and she'd be on her way home.

She ran damp fingers through the long brown mane and

shook it, letting it fall in shimmering waves. She usually wore it loose at work, curling softly around her shoulders. It was thick, and although she was nearing twenty-eight, she still hadn't found any silver hair in the shiny mass— though she looked for it carefully. She reapplied her lipstick and cinched the wide leather belt around her waist a notch tighter before heading back onto the floor.

The rest of the afternoon passed smoothly, until the incoming team relieved Angela and her partner.

As she was leaving, she checked the black box on her supervisor's desk, looking, as she had for the past week, for the Familiarization flight tickets she had requested.

"Looking for your FAM ticket, Lawrey?" Looking over the top of his glasses, Bob Haskell reminded Angela of her Phase Four training instructor in Oklahoma. The toughest instructor in the training center, he'd also been the one from whom she had learned the most. He demanded perfection from his students and weeded out those who couldn't make the grade.

"Yes. It's not here yet."

"I understand you had a little excitement today." Bob tipped his chair back until it balanced on two legs and trained his gaze on the young woman.

"I'd like to throttle the guy who pulled that stunt," she answered. "That Westair pilot handled it, though."

"Good work, Lawrey."

She walked through the room that hummed with the sound of low voices and sophisticated equipment, and pushed through the double doors that isolated the control room from the rest of the center. Already, she was looking forward to a shower and a swim in her condo's pool, then a quiet evening at home. Alone.

She swung her Mercedes convertible through the north gate and onto the highway that faced an unequaled view of Long's Peak. Rocky spires at the top of the 14,000 foot mountain looked as ethereal as wind-whipped clouds of snow. She breathed deeply the fresh air that still held a trace of winter. Angela had never regretted her decision to move to Colorado. After the extensive training session in Oklahoma and finishing top in her class, she requested the one open slot in the prestigious Denver Center in Longmont, Colorado. Noted for its top-notch instructors and incomparable small-town feel, the Longmont facility fulfilled all of the young controller's expectations. She hoped to stay there forever.

It was March. But springtime in the Rockies meant days in the sixties, nights in the thirties and weather changes that brought snow as easily as sunshine. In two weeks, she was due for some time off, and she would be vacationing for the first time, which was something she eagerly anticipated. Angela exercised with an aggressive cross-training routine of jogging, swimming and weights. But lately she spent more time in the pool, not only to feel comfortable in her two-piece bathing suit, but to prepare for the snorkeling she planned in Kauai.

The rest of the week dragged. Every day Angela checked the black box on the manager's desk for her tickets to paradise, and every day she was disappointed—with only one week left. On the following Friday afternoon, the team supervisor called a routine "crew break-out," and she and her coworkers gathered in an upstairs meeting room to air complaints, receive new schedules and directives, and to ask questions.

After the briefing, Bob Haskell unfolded an official-looking letter and announced, "Last week we had an inci-

dent that came much too close to becoming front-page
news. I don't need to remind you that we've had our share
of bad press lately. Every controller dreads the kind of
news that leaves families severed and lives lost. We live
with that danger every day—you know that. It was a combination of skill, quick action and luck on the part of the
pilot and the controller that averted disaster. Today we have
the opportunity to congratulate one of our youngest employees. What I have here is the FAA's Outstanding Flight
Assist Award, for being recognized as one of the best. Ms.
Lawrey, please step forward."

Angela and Richie exchanged glances as she stood. She
could feel her face begin to heat, knowing she was blushing
from the unexpected attention. Most of the crowd clapped
as she moved toward the front of the room. She hadn't
known about the award, and Angela was unaccustomed to
singular recognition.

Haskell shook her hand, handed her a certificate, and
continued. "In addition, the recipient is awarded $1,000 for
receiving this national honor." Haskell read the letter of
commendation, signed by the president of Westair upon
recommendation by Captain Robert "Chip" Stephens.

So that's his name, Angela mused. She wasn't likely to
forget a name like *Chip.* Haskell handed her the letter along
with the check, then prompted applause to congratulate Angela Lawrey on her accomplishment. The meeting broke
up, and several of Angela's coworkers shook her hand and
slapped her on the back for a job well-done.

Richie waited for Angela, his lanky frame leaning
against the wall, arms folded and legs crossed at the ankle.
His straight red hair hung diagonally over his forehead. He
reminded Angela of a ten-year-old in a schoolyard. Richie
was her sounding board and support, the partner with whom

she worked best. They walked out together past a stone-faced Sam Rankin, who acknowledged them with a curt nod.

"Man, he's a cold duck," Richie whispered after they'd passed. "He gives me the creeps. It's like he's just waiting to pounce the minute I screw up."

Angela snickered. "You're right, so make sure you don't."

"So what are you going to do with the dough? We could throw one heck of a party."

"Dream on, Richie." Angela smiled. "I still don't believe it," she said, shaking her head.

"I should be so lucky," Richie grumbled. "You got an award, a fat check and a date out of a little tête-à-tête in the sky."

"And the part you hate the most is that I got a date, right?"

"Hmmph. He's probably old enough to be your father, married six times, and can't afford a drive-through."

"You ought to practice some positive visualization, Richie. It works, you know."

"If that's what you use, I guess I should. Seems like you have all the luck."

As they passed by the area supervisor's desk, Angela stopped once again to check the box. She separated the dividers, then saw it. "All right! My tickets."

Richie checked the envelope she held. "Hawaii, huh?"

"Here I come," she added. "Beaches, sunshine—"

"Bikinis . . ." Richie moaned. "Why didn't I think of that?"

"You can request it too, you know." Angela smiled. "Westair and Universal fly out everyday."

"I can't this year. I've already taken my FAM trips on their airlines. I'll have to wait for next year."

"Too bad," she teased. "I'll send you a postcard."

"Don't. I couldn't stand the pain. When are you leaving?"

"Monday. I'll have two days off this weekend and then I'll be gone for four glorious days."

Richie opened the door for her as she swept through. Her hair swished with the same carefree flow as her georgette dress. She felt ten pounds lighter since she'd received the award and the FAM tickets had finally arrived.

"You're happy," Richie observed glumly.

"You bet. I'm looking forward to this time off. You behave while I'm gone, Richie. Don't miss me too much." She stood on her toes and pecked Richie on his freckled cheek with sisterly affection. "Remember—positive visualization!"

Smoothing the white skirt over her hips, Angela checked every angle of her appearance in the mirror. The FAM trip instructions stated that female participants were to dress in business attire. The young woman who stood before the mirror took that order literally: she had chosen this suit because it wouldn't wrinkle on the long flight, and looked as starchy and sophisticated as an executive in a Denver skyscraper.

The cotton shell she wore had an embroidered flowery design that lent an exquisitely feminine touch to the suit. Once packed and ready to leave, Angela drew on a matching jacket, pulling the softly-rolled collar up on her neck. It was a summer-weight design that would be perfect for the balmy weather she expected upon arrival in Honolulu.

Today she wore her thick brown hair pulled into a French twist on the back of her head.

Angela drove the forty-five minutes to Denver, arriving in time to check in at passenger reservations an hour early. The Westair employee at the ticket counter directed her to wait upstairs at the airline's flight deck, which was inaccessible to the ordinary traveler. Her hands were moist in anticipation of the trip, knowing her ticket could be canceled without warning, or she could be "bumped" at the last minute. She nervously paced the flight deck, hoping luck was with her.

After what seemed like forever, Angela heard the boarding call. The crew was seated and the boarding procedure began. Minutes passed. When it was clear her ticket was secured, Angela boarded.

An attractive blond flight attendant opened the cockpit door for Angela and pointed out her seat. There was just enough room for four people in the cramped area, so the attendant stuck her head through the opening.

"Gentlemen, we have a controller onboard today." She pointed to the man in the rear. "Tom Parry, navigator . . ."

Smiling, the uniformed officer nodded. Then the copilot turned around. "Harvey Andrews." He smiled, extending his hand.

The captain appeared to be listening to the headset, unaware of her presence until his copilot elbowed him and pointed in her direction with his thumb. He slid the headset off saying, "Nice perfume, Lou-ise," as he turned and discovered they had a guest.

"And our illustrious captain, Chip Stephens," the stewardess announced. A teasing lilt in her voice. "What was your name, Ms.—"

Angela gasped when she realized who the pilot was. And

she wasn't prepared for the riveting blue eyes that met hers when he faced her.

"An-gela. Law-rey," she stammered.

"AG?" the captain verified.

Angela nodded and met his surprised gaze with her own.

His polite smile turned into an explosion of white teeth and words, "Well, if it ain't my guardian *AN-GEL!*" The captain reached out and pumped the young woman's hand. "Am I glad to meet you!"

The stewardess snickered and closed the door, leaving a flabbergasted Angela encased with the Southern gentleman and his cohorts.

"Boys, did I ever tell you about the time I was flying into DIA, got my clearance to descend from this heavenly voice from above, then wham-o. All of a sudden I've got a puddle jumper in the middle of my flight path. We-l-l-l," he drawled, stretching the word to emphasize the story. "That same angel from above started shooting orders like my Naval instructor from Fallon."

The crew laughed.

"That's Colorado for you. If it's not those front range winds, it's those front range desk jockeys tryin' to play pilot." Captain Stephens embellished the story, showing how the little plane tore right across the field into his path.

Angela noted the long, tapered fingers that he flourished in the air as he demonstrated how he had angled his plane up, following her orders, and banked to the right to maneuver his jet stream out of the little plane's way.

She also noticed his tanned face and the lines that grew around his eyes whenever he smiled. He wasn't dark haired as she had imagined him to be when she heard his voice over the air; his hair was sandy blond. He had the face of experience and an aquiline nose above sensuous lips. Lips, she'd bet, that had kissed hundreds of women.

No wonder the stewardess introduced him the way she had. No doubt all the female employees of Westair had come under Captain Stephens's scrutiny and sugar-sweet flattery.

His gaze roved over her without restraint, from the top of her French twist to the low heels of her white pumps. His blue eyes glittered with unmasked admiration. *She's better-looking in person than I had imagined her—even looks like an angel.* "Well this is my lucky day!"

His comment startled Angela out of her study of the magnetic pilot. Tom and Harvey chuckled, leaving Angela with the feeling she had made an impression on this flight crew, thanks to the welcome Captain Chip Stephens had provided.

"I feel safer already," he finished, "now that I've got my guardian angel on board. Shall we go, fellas?" Harvey buckled himself in, adjusted his headgear and scanned his list.

Angela sensed the mood shift from jovial to serious as the men gave the job at hand their undivided attention. Not unlike her profession, the gravity of their responsibility never allowed for casualness when it was time to focus.

She watched with fascination as Harvey called out each item from the check-off list, and Chip switched each lever followed by, "Check." In just a few minutes they had verified that each one of the gauges, switches, and levers were operational.

Captain Stephens' face reflected the seriousness of his duty. No doubt, Angela presumed, a result of the intense military training he had referred to.

"Let's get this bird off the ground," Stephens ordered, and gave a thumbs-up to the ground crew.

Angela smiled, remembering Richie's guess about the Captain. Unlike Richie had imagined him, Chip appeared to be in his mid to late thirties. No more. He had a youthful exuberance about him that, coupled with experience, gave him the command and reflexes he needed to pull off the kind of maneuver he had two weeks ago.

It had been two weeks to the day, she realized. They were now on his return trip home from that same afternoon flight.

As if he knew what she was thinking, the captain turned around and winked at her. Angela didn't know how to take his obvious flirting. Maybe that was just his way, but she would've felt less vulnerable had she been dressed in a pantsuit that would not emphasize her femininity.

Captain Stephens grinned, then turned to look out his window at their progress, as the airplane's tug pushed them back away from the concourse.

After they had been cleared for takeoff, Angela settled into the small seat and mentally prepared herself for the long flight ahead. Since the trip was a mandatory job requirement, she had prepared a list of questions to ask the captain and crew regarding their aircraft and its capabilities. A report was expected at the end of the trip, and Angela would have it typed and ready to submit upon her return.

To Angela, every aspect of her job was serious. It was the way she worked. She had a job to do, and she did it to the best of her ability. The young woman waited until the crew settled into a more relaxed state as they cruised over the Rockies before she began her interrogation. She was familiar with many of the gauges in the 747, as she had seen them in other aircraft.

Since her expertise dealt mainly with the heavy traffic in and around Denver, she was unfamiliar with the flight procedures outside of her area. First Officer Andrews answered her technical questions, and the navigator answered her weather concerns. Captain Stephens asked more questions of her than she did of him regarding the operations of the Denver Center.

They were all interested in the updated computer system that Denver Center had acquired. Angela was familiar with its operation, and eagerly rattled off statistics and figures that she had memorized as part of her intensive training.

A few minutes later they encountered a minimum amount of turbulence as they flew over Vail and Aspen, then angled toward the Black Canyon near Gunnison, Colorado.

Captain Stephens proved to be sensitive and courteous, in spite of his boisterous introduction, making her feel welcome and comfortable. Officer Andrews and Parry seemed to withdraw from the conversation as Captain Stephens directed it to a more personal vein.

"So where are you bound, Angel?" he asked. "I'm off for the day once we land in L.A. How about that dinner I promised you?"

Angela had already fallen for the Captain's easy manner and Southern charm. She wished now that she had arranged for a few hours layover in Los Angeles, but she hadn't.

"I've got to catch the Westair flight at seven-forty. I'm going to Hawaii—Kauai as a matter of fact."

"Kauai? All by yourself?"

His question created a stirring in her stomach that she was unaccustomed to. *Why didn't it bother me when the men at work asked? Get hold of yourself, Lawrey.* She hated to admit to this man that she was going there alone.

"I'm taking it easy," she answered. "I'm mostly planning to sunbathe and sleep."

Chip knew better than to respond to that. He could only imagine what she looked like in a bathing suit. He'd love to join her sunning on the beach, or cavorting in the waves with the warm, salty water splashing over their bodies.

She is smart. And what a mind. And beautiful. Knock it off, Stephens. You're acting like a teenager.

"Well, I don't know about you boys, but Hawaii sounds good to me. How 'bout if we refuel this bird and detour to Honolulu?"

Andrews and Parry cheered at that idea, and unanimously placed Angela in charge.

Angela listened to each man's stories about their individual close-calls. Before long, they had entered Los Angeles airspace and, once again, reverted to business.

It was a textbook landing. As the passengers deplaned, Angela thanked the crew and shook hands with each. When Captain Stephens grasped her hand, it was with a warmth and electricity that was far removed from the exuberance she had experienced before. His eyes were a deep shade of blue, like that of the sky when darkness melts into the horizon.

She rose to leave.

"Hold on, Angel," Captain Stephens said, gathering his flattop hat. "I'll walk you to your gate."

Chapter Two

Angela felt her face flush as she realized the man was going with her. After all the passengers had disembarked, the stewardess retrieved Angela's purse from the staff stowage area and handed it to her. Captain Stephens escorted Angela from the aircraft.

"You've got about an hour, right?" he asked.

"Yes, but—"

"What time does your flight take off?"

"Seven-forty."

"There's a little pub around here where we can wait, or I could take you to our officers' lounge if you'd prefer."

Angela hesitated for a moment. "The latter sounds a bit more inviting, if you don't mind."

"Mind?" he drawled. "Honey, I'd take you to Toledo if that's where you wanted to go."

"I just meant, there's probably less noise, and all—"

Chip smiled. "Lots less commotion, darlin'. And I'd like to get to know you a little."

16

Angela felt herself blush involuntarily.

"You know—shop talk," he added. "That kind of thing."

Angela hoped he could be trusted. *He is more than attractive*, she decided. *He's devastating.* Her gaze wandered to his left hand. *He doesn't wear a wedding band. Is he like so many men I've met who prefer not to advertise their relationship, or is he truly single? He doesn't act married.*

Chip led the way to the Westair lounge, reserved for officers and attendants between flights. With a flurry of button-pushing he unlocked the door, then held it open for her.

A series of bay windows faced the ocean, providing a spectacular view of the Pacific. From this vantage point, Angela watched as two planes came in from the west to land.

"May I take your jacket?"

"I'm fine, thanks," she said, settling on the pale leather couch.

Chip wandered to the back of the room, where a bar and stools apparently camouflaged a trove of glassware and a refrigerator.

"Drink?" he offered.

"No—" Angela began to decline until she eyed the two cans of soda he balanced between two ice-filled glasses.

"Diet ginger ale okay?"

"Sure."

"I'll bet you don't imbibe caffeine, do you?"

"As little as possible," she admitted. Angela was a little surprised by his astute deduction. She had declined cola in the cockpit in deference to the clear carbonated drink, but she hadn't realized he was listening.

"Thank you." She accepted the drink from his outstretched hand.

"Don't smoke, no caffeine . . ." he added. "What else don't you do?" That boyish sparkle lit his eyes and Angela's stomach flip-flopped. He had a way of making her feel vulnerable even though he was seated about three feet away.

She liked what she saw of Captain Chip Stephens, and it was no secret he was attracted to her. If she was inclined to date, Chip was an attractive choice.

"Is your real name Chip, or is that just a nickname?"

"Well," he drawled. "I don't like to talk about that."

"Oh? Why not? You don't like your name?"

"My middle name is Dale," he explained.

"How'd they get Chip out of that?"

"I went out dancing one night with the stewardesses," he grinned then swigged his drink. "You figure it out."

Angela watched as the man in front of her blushed. His cheeks flamed and the tell-tale flush spread to his neck.

Angela made the connection. "You like to dance?"

"I plead the fifth."

They both laughed. It seemed to Angela that whatever shyness she should be feeling was out of order. Bolstered by his honesty, she continued. "Are you . . . married?"

"Would I act like I was fallin' in love for the first time if I was, Angel?"

"I don't know. But I expect a straight answer."

"Nope." He grinned, and looked at her from over the top of his glass as he drank deeply.

"Engaged? Attached?"

"Nope on all counts. You?"

Angela shook her head and smiled. "I'm single, unattached, and on my way to Hawaii."

Chip whistled softly through his teeth. "What I wouldn't give to be a native right now." A wisp of hair had escaped her coiffure, and he gently tucked it behind her ear. "What about that dinner I promised you?"

"I've got a plane to catch."

"I wish you didn't have to go."

"I've been waiting for this trip for *weeks*."

"So, will you be flying with me on the return leg?"

Angela almost choked on her drink. "I—I don't know. I could look at my ticket."

"What day is it?"

"I'll be flying back on Friday."

"No such luck." He breathed a heavy sigh. "I believe I'm scheduled off that day."

He seemed disappointed. Angela liked that his expressions so clearly mirrored his thoughts. *What a charmer.*

Captain Stephens checked his watch. "Westair is very proud of its reputation for punctuality. It's about time to catch that plane, isn't it?"

Angela placed her drink on the table and stood.

"I don't know what it is about you, lady, but you make me feel like we're the only two people in the world."

"Chip," Angela chided. "You are the most unbelievable character."

"What do you mean?"

"I can't tell if your flattery is sincere or if—"

"An-gel," Chip moved close to her, but Angela didn't budge. He drew her hand to his lips and gently kissed her fingers. "I mean every word."

His whisper sparked a flame inside her that she knew would keep her warm all the way to Hawaii. He turned to open the door, offering her his hand. Although she had just met him, Angela longed to be with this man. An aching emptiness gathered inside and she realized it would be a long, lonely four days in Kauai.

* * *

Angela stood at the open hotel window and gazed at the jade-colored sea. Miles of white sand stretched in either direction, and very few people werc out. Only couples, walking hand-in-hand beneath the canopy of trees that lined the sidewalk. Was Captain Stephens looking out at the ocean, as she was at the moment? Or was he arranging dinner with someone else?

Turning back to the room, she idly picked up her purse from the bed and placed it on the dresser. She stood on one foot and leaned over to remove her shoe, then switched feet to remove the other. Carefully, she placed them side by side in the small, open closet.

Hanalei Hotel was a quaint, charming establishment built in the Twenties. There were no phones or televisions in the small rooms. Just one concession had been made to accommodate today's tourists: two modern queen-size beds fit snugly in the room where, she was sure, a massive antique four-poster had once stood. The brochure boasted of the "modern" furnishings in many of the rooms. It was the owners' answer to attracting out-of-the-way tourists like Angela who chose to avoid the busier islands of Oahu, Hawaii, and Maui for the less-populated Kauai.

She began to wonder if she had made a mistake. A bustling, too-busy beach scene might have done more to distract her preoccupation with the exciting pilot, than the solitude and restful atmosphere of this old island town with its isolated beaches.

Angela eyed the beds with disdain. She would have preferred a single four-poster. Glancing at her mournful expression in the oval mirror above the dresser she asked her reflection, "What's the matter with you? You fly three thousand miles to heaven on earth and then stand around feeling sorry for yourself. You're out of it, Lawrey."

She whisked the combs from her hair and let it tumble onto her shoulders. Shaking the bends and kinks from it, she combed her fingers through its heavy weight.

Angela scurried across the hardwood floor into the refuge of the tiny bathroom. She turned on the shower and stepped inside the stall to meet a blast of water. She tried adjusting the shower head for a softer spray, but found it was also a relic from seventy years ago. It wouldn't budge.

"This was your idea," she reminded herself. She felt herself becoming more depressed by the minute.

The shower revived her somewhat, but Angela still felt dull and disoriented. Her growling stomach reminded her she hadn't eaten since the light meal she'd been served on the plane.

It was a little past ten P.M. island time, four hours earlier than Colorado. She pulled on a coral-colored pantsuit, emptied the contents of her purse into a multi-colored woven bag and headed out the door.

The narrow hallway led to an open, winding staircase that poured into the lobby. She grasped the cool mahogany wood of the banister. Miniature, potted palm trees decorated the spacious room in oversized clay pots, along with bouquets of exotic flowers that perfumed the air. Square terracotta tiles shimmered beneath the evening lights.

As she descended to the ground floor, she heard the clerk say, "There she is now."

Angela looked in the direction from which the voice came.

"Chip!"

Surprise carried her cry across the lobby as he rushed to meet her.

Strong arms encircled her as he lifted and twirled her in his grasp. When he set her down, the room continued to spin.

"Hi, darlin'," he said, kissing her cheek. "I was just telling this young man that my wife had probably already checked in."

"Your *wife?*"

He buried his face in her hair and whispered. "Trust me." Turning to the young man, he said, "Would you please have my bag taken to the room?" Then, loudly enough to be heard by the clerk, he announced, "You must be starved, waiting for me like you did. Come on, let's go eat."

Entwining their arms, Chip guided her through the lobby. He snatched a scarlet hibiscus bloom from an arrangement and slipped it behind her ear as they strolled out into the night air. When they reached the sidewalk, he stopped and pulled her into his arms, kissing her again.

"What are you doing here?" she asked.

"I came to see you. You don't mind, do you?"

"Well, no, but—"

"You were hard to find. You didn't say where you were staying."

"I didn't expect to be trailed. What's this business about your wife?"

His grin was devastating, coupled with the fire in his eyes.

"It seems the hotel is booked. You had to pick the smallest one on the island, didn't you?"

"The oldest, too," she added mournfully. "I thought it would be fun. Charming. And old-fashioned."

"And booked solid," he repeated.

"Where are you going to stay?"

"With you."

"You can't! I made reservations two months ago. They wouldn't—"

"You don't want me to stay with you?"

"What?"

"I promise." He held two fingers up in the Boy Scout sign and pasted an innocent-looking expression on his face. "I was a Boy Scout before I was a pilot."

Angela snickered. "You've got some explaining to do, Captain."

"You haven't made dinner reservations, have you?"

"No. I thought I'd take a walk and see what's available."

"Good. I know just the place."

"So you're also a tour guide?"

"Since about five minutes ago, honey. Come on."

Chip guided them toward a low-roofed café. A flickering neon sign announced *Shanty Jack's*. After trudging through the sand to reach its oceanfront entrance, they stepped inside. A native host ushered them to a table on the far side of the darkened room. Each circular table was decorated with a candle housed inside a mottled glass globe. The bar and stage were brightly lit, and a lacquered wood dance floor was crowded to capacity with couples swinging to loud vintage rock 'n roll.

"This is your idea of a restaurant?" Angela shouted above the music.

"They have a great seafood platter. You like fish, don't you?"

"Love it," Angela shouted.

After the band finished their song, a gregarious crowd cheered and clapped until the music started again. A slower, softer song began.

"Welcome to *Shanty Jack's*." The waitress wore a colorful sarong that wrapped her in a brightly-patterned floral print. She smiled, waiting to take their order.

Chip requested tropical punch and two seafood platters, then turned his attention to his companion.

"You're a long way from home, aren't you, sailor?" Angela teased.

"I got shore leave. Took time off for good behavior."

"Really, Chip. You can't just walk off the job like that, can you?"

"I had some time coming and I took it. After you left, I couldn't have operated a toy train, much less a jumbo jet. You knocked the wind out of my sails, Angel." The quivering flame of the candle cast a faint light on his face. "I wanted to get to know you better, and I figured this was the perfect time to do it." His thumb smoothed over her knuckles, sending electric impulses up her arm. "Wanna dance?"

Angela rose trance-like as he pulled out her chair. She circled her arms around his neck and pressed her head against his chest as they swayed to the hypnotic music. She felt the steady beating of his heart, and wondered if he was as deeply affected by her as she was by him. The thought warmed her all over.

She raised her face and their lips met in a gentle kiss. She was unaware that the music had stopped until they were jarred by someone leaving the floor. The next song was a rendition of the slow tune, *Earth Angel.*

"They're playing our song," he whispered.

She closed her eyes and let the music take her into the fantasy she had created. Everything around her disappeared as she became an extension of him. His cologne was headier to her than the hibiscus he had tucked behind her ear.

"Hmm-mm-mm, *earth angel, earth angel, will you be mine?*" Chip sang.

"You're crazy." Angela combed her fingers through his hair. "Deliciously mad."

He swung her low as the song ended and then raised her. "Madly in love," he stated as he led the way back to their table.

The evening was a blend of island magic and allure. They ate seven kinds of seafood and toasted to romance. Angela laughed freely while Chip entertained her with tales of people he'd met in the States and abroad. They stayed until the restaurant closed. Although she hadn't slept in twenty-four hours, Angela felt alive with excitement. Tonight was a continuance of the dream that began yesterday morning when she left home, and it wasn't going to end. Captain Stephens had become the object of her vacation fantasy.

"Let's walk back along the beach," Chip suggested. "How does that sound?"

They slipped off their shoes, swinging them as they walked arm-in-arm along the shore. Plodding through the soft pockets of sand was a feat in itself until they reached the smooth, hard-packed earth where the ocean washed the beach in its tides. The ground felt cool and damp beneath her bare feet, and the waves that rushed in as if playing tag, broke over her ankles and dampened the turned cuffs of her pants.

He looked relaxed wearing an open-necked shirt tucked inside white twill trousers. His jacket lay draped over his shoulder, and he carried his shoes in one hand. His other arm was securely fastened around Angela's waist in a warmly possessive manner.

"I can't believe you're here," she murmured.

"I can't believe I'm with you. I've never chased a lady halfway across the ocean before."

"How'd you manage to get a flight out so quickly?"

"I have friends in high places." He smiled and kissed her on the nose. "I'm glad you weren't on your way to the moon. That would've been a little more difficult to arrange."

Ghostly-looking gulls scuttled out of their way, as the two made a beeline for a sandy perch at the edge of the beach. Sheltered slightly by a grassy mound, he arranged his jacket and motioned Angela to sit on it. He leaned against the bank, and drew her backward. She scooted between his legs and rested her arms on his raised knees.

"Fun?" he asked.

"It's great. I'm glad you're here. When I got to the hotel and realized this was more a romantic getaway than a singles haven, I thought I was in trouble." Angela sighed.

"Little did you know I was hot on your trail." He pulled her closer.

"What if I'd been meeting some hot-shot controller, and arranged this rendezvous with someone else?" She peered over her shoulder, trying to make out the expression on his moonlit face.

"Angel, the way you looked at me when I left you at the gate . . ." He sighed heavily. "You're lucky I didn't haul you out of there caveman-style to my apartment."

Angela felt a sudden flush of heat shoot up her neck to the roots of her hair. She didn't realize that he saw the revealing look on her face. Now that he was with her, what was she going to do? And he had invited himself to share her room at the hotel. What kind of charisma did this man possess?

"What are you thinking about?"

"You."

"I'll bet you're thinking I do this regularly aren't you?" Chip asked.

"The thought had crossed my mind."

"I thought so."

"The stewardess gave me that impression when we were introduced. I suspect your marital status precedes your reputation as a pilot, Captain Stephens."

"Now don't you go thinkin' I'm some kind of playboy pilot, Angel. I'll admit I'm not a saint, but I haven't had a serious relationship since little Bobby Ray was born.

"Bobby Ray?"

"My son."

"I thought you weren't married?"

"I'm not now. I was once . . . a long time ago. Rayanne and I were high school sweethearts. Married right after graduation. Bobby Ray was less than a year old when she died. Car accident. Seventeen years ago, now." He sighed.

Angela's senses roused to full alert as she detected the change in his tone. Although she wanted to know more about his past, she could hear the pain etched in his voice.

"You don't have to talk about it, if you don't want to."

"Like I said . . . it was a long time ago." He rubbed her cheek softly with his thumb. "My mama, Pops and I raised little Bobby Ray. It took me a long time to get over it. He doesn't remember her, of course."

His voice sounded heavy and distant.

"I'm sorry," Angela soothed. "It must have been hard."

"Ah, we got by. Bobby Ray's graduating from high school this year. He's a good boy . . . I mean, man. Heck, he's almost eighteen already. Almost the same age I was when he was born." Chip smoothed his hands over Angela's arms then folded his arms over hers. He felt her shiver. "Cold?"

"No." Angela snuggled closer against him and drew her knees to her chest. "It feels good just to sit here."

Nuzzling the back of her hair, he inhaled deeply. Mingled with the sea-salt air, her hair smelled clean and lemony. He rested his chin on her head and peered out at the rolling waves. Angela had rekindled a flame in his soul he'd thought long ago extinguished.

"Do you believe in fate?" he murmured.

"Not really." She leaned her head back against his shoulder. "I abandoned daydreams when I was a little girl. My dad taught me the world is made up of facts, figures and hard knocks. That didn't allow for much foolishness."

"And that's why you became a controller?" he asked.

"I suppose so. It suits me. Fate has nothing to do with reality. You make your decisions or let someone else make them for you. Fate is someone's excuse for not having control over themselves."

"What about love?" he asked, rocking her gently in the cocoon he'd formed around her.

"That's something I don't know too much about." Angela sighed dreamily. "But I'm willing to learn."

"Do you ever think about being married?"

"No. I don't think I'm ready. Or maybe I haven't met the right guy yet." She elbowed him playfully.

"Yet?"

"It's a little early to tell, don't you think?"

"No better time than the present. I happen to know a really nice guy—"

"I'll bet you do, Captain." She snuggled against his shoulder. "Why is it?"

"What?"

"I'm not afraid of you."

"Of course you aren't. I have thousands of people's lives in my hands every day. If you can't trust a pilot, who can you trust?"

"I didn't mean it that way, and you know it." She lowered her head into the groove at the base of his neck and listened to the steady beating of his heart. She could feel his pulse quicken. He felt so good against her. She felt as comfortable as if they were a married couple watching the Sunday football game, rather than the strangers they were, watching waves break on the shore.

Trade winds scudded across the beach and showered a small spray of sand upon them. The ocean roared and splashed, lashing out rhythmically at the ancient earth.

"Want to know a secret?" Chip whispered.

"Yes."

"It's four in the morning."

"Mmm . . ." she burrowed her head into his shoulder. "It doesn't feel like it."

"Are you one of those night owls who stays up all night and sleeps all day?"

"Sometimes . . . when we're on swing shifts."

"Well . . ." he said, rising to his feet and dusting the sand off the back of his trousers. "I get up pretty early in the morning."

"Even when you're on vacation?" She took the hand he offered.

"Who says I'm on vacation?"

"Well, I—aren't you?"

"Chasing women is a full-time occupation, Ms. Lawrey. One I don't take lightly."

He pecked her on her forehead and ducked when she swung playfully at him.

The two ran down the beach, Chip staying a few feet out of her reach until he turned and tackled her. Locking her in his embrace, they rolled on the pillowy sand.

"Don't believe it." He laughed and squeezed her. "Angela, honey," he whispered in his sweet Southern drawl. "I've never shadowed a woman in my life 'til now. And I'm not about to let you go."

Angela scrambled to her feet and brushed off the sand that clung to her pants. Sweeping her hair to the side, she grabbed a handful and shook the sand from it. Moist air caused her hair to wave in unruly curls, unlike the sleek coiffure she had worn the day before.

"It's almost daybreak." She sighed, noting the thin line of crimson on the watery eastern horizon.

The sky remained an inky black where the moon had no sovereignty. Only the beach, stark and white, reflected the subdued glow of the pale globe that hung in the sky. The frilly edge of foam that danced on the waves looked iridescent as it splashed and changed forms into myriad patterns.

"Let's turn in," Chip said. They walked in rhythm, close together.

They ascended the steps of the sweeping stairway, and Angela led the way to her room. The old brass key she held unlocked the door. When she switched on the light, the room was bathed in a garish blast of bright, modern lights.

She watched as he hung the *Do Not Disturb* sign on the ornate door handle and latched the chain, locking them inside.

Angela sat on the pale chenille bedspread on the bed closest to the bathroom, wordlessly eyeing her roommate.

"Two beds?" He crossed the room and hung his jacket on a straight-backed vanity chair.

She became self-conscious and wondered what she should do next. Did he think they would only be occupying one?

Chip chuckled and unbuttoned his shirt.

"I'll be just a moment," she said, making her exit into the bathroom.

A few minutes later, Angela emerged from the bathroom blotting her hair wearing a fluffy white terry cloth robe.

"What's this?" She tugged at the corner of a queen-sized sheet strung up between the beds.

Chip's head popped over the top of the flimsy barrier. "Sh-h-h, you'll wake the neighbors."

"What are you doing?"

"Pretty ingenious, huh?" he asked, grinning. Half-dressed, he wore navy blue silk pajama bottoms. His shoulders and arms were tanned and muscular. It was obvious to Angela that he took care of himself and cared about his appearance.

He pulled her in his arms and kissed her. "I didn't want you to think I had other plans. Do you like it?"

"I . . . I don't know." She tugged at one corner of the sheet and inspected the line.

"You don't see the wall to my adjoining suite?"

"Is that what it is? Where'd you get the fishing line?"

"I brought my pole with me, just in case . . ."

"In case what?"

"In case I missed you and had nothing else to do." He gathered her in his arms. "Listen," he whispered. "I want to court you properly. It's something I like to do when I fall in love."

"And how often is that?"

"So far, once every two decades." He kissed the tip of her nose. "I want to do this right, and if I rush in like a bomber on target, you might think I was only after your more physical attributes."

"You're not?"

Chip looked skeptical. "How do I know you're not just amusing yourself with *me*?"

"You don't know that, do you?" Angela teased.

"Maybe this wasn't such a good idea. Three nights with you." Chip growled, playfully pecking her on the nose. "Good night, Angel."

"But—"

"Hush now," he quieted her. "Go to sleep and dream sweet dreams."

Angela gazed after him, astonished, as Chip made his way to the bathroom. She snuggled down into the soft cotton sheets and lifted a manicured finger to the "wall" between their beds. It was the last thing she remembered as she smiled deeply, then fell asleep.

Chapter Three

In the moments between waking and dreaming, Angela thought she heard a rooster crowing. She felt a gentle breeze caressing her face like a silken fan, and listened to the soft rustle of fabric flapping in the dreamy distance. The young woman's thoughts immersed her in a loving, nostalgic feeling as dreams moved her backward in time. She saw herself a child again pressing the clean, crisp sheet to her face, as her mother hung laundry on an outdoor line. Slowly, Angela opened sleepy eyes to greet a pearl gray sky.

When she realized where she was, she sat up and awoke fully to a queen-size sheet brushing gently over her face. A rooster crowed, louder this time. She hadn't imagined it. She swept the sheet away with her forearm, smiling as she recalled why it was there. She drew the sheet aside and peered at her companion. Captain Stephens still slept soundly. He lay sprawled on his queen-size bed with one arm curved over his eyes.

Angela donned her terry cloth robe and padded over to his side of the room. Leaning over his sleeping face, she kissed his closed eyes, mouth and nose.

"Mmm," he murmured. "Have I died and gone to heaven?"

Angela moved a blond lock of hair from his forehead with the tip of her finger. "Good morning, handsome."

"It's true, I have. Not only does my angel speak, but she's real."

Angela's dark hair formed a curtain around them as she kissed him.

"I thought you were asleep." She studied the bright blue eyes that glittered recklessly.

"I was dreaming about this gorgeous, sweet female and then I woke up and found out I wasn't dreaming at all . . ."

Outside, gulls wheeled and railed as the turquoise waves rolled and crashed and hissed at the shoreline. The sky was a carpet of fluffy white clouds that played hide and seek with the sun and bathed the earth in gigantic dots of shade and sunlight.

"Shall we call room service for breakfast?" Captain Stephens checked his watch. "Better make that lunch."

"No. Let's eat out. I'll race you to the shower," she teased, and dashed into the cubicle.

"Make it quick, lady," he called through the door. "Or I'll be forced to join you."

Navy blue duck pants and a pale blue shirt complemented Chip's coloring and enhanced the deep blue eyes that he trained on Angela. She struggled to fasten the clasp on her necklace until Chip took over the task. That done, he watched her in the mirror as she brushed her hair and twisted it into a thick knot which she secured with a comb on the crown of her head.

Chip guided her chair back from the vanity and offered his hand to Angela, allowing her to rise with graceful precision. His gaze wandered from her face to the fitted bodice and flared skirt, down to the open sandals on her feet. "You look lovely, Angela. Your mama must've been a beauty."

"My father evidently thought so," Angela replied. "But I think I favor his side of the family." She looked in the mirror again. It surprised her to realize that perhaps she did resemble her mother, after all.

"Where do your parents live?" Chip asked.

"Dad's in Nebraska. My mother lives in Kansas City."

"Do you see them often?"

"Not really. I've been so wrapped up with my training and then working full-time—visiting family wasn't on the schedule."

"I get home every couple of weeks or so," Chip confessed. "I couldn't live without Mama's home-cookin'. You'd like her. She and Pops have lived in that same house since they married."

"Where?"

"They live on a ranch outside San Antonio. The nearest town is Mountain Home."

"That's where you grew up?"

"Yep." Chip's blue eyes riveted on her.

She felt the heat from his gaze, and wondered how she had lived so long without him. *Is this what being in love is like? If it is, maybe it isn't all bad.*

They left the room to lunch at a small café. Chip and Angela strolled through a park under the shade of ancient banyan trees. A brass marker identified the largest of them as five hundred years old.

A wooden pier stretched out fifty feet into the water, where several locals and tourists tried their hand at fishing. "That's where I usually hang out," Chip said, pointing in the distance.

"I had no idea you'd been here before. You didn't mention it on the plane."

"I don't like to give away my secrets. I've been here lots of times. I knew when you said you were going to Kauai we had more than coincidence here. Why Kauai and not the other islands?"

"I didn't want to spend it with swarms of tourists. I thought this island might give me a better feel for Hawaii as it was in the past."

"So that's why you picked the Hanalei instead of one of the major hotels?"

"Yes. I'm big on old-fashioned things."

"Me too," Chip squeezed her. "Like old-fashioned dates, old-fashioned strolls through the park, old-fashioned love affairs . . ."

Angela laughed along with him at his reference to their relationship. It was wonderful being with Chip, but she was already thinking about how it would end. She wasn't fool enough to think they had a workable situation. What little time they had together they shared right now.

"How long are you staying, Chip?"

"Until you leave."

"Really?"

"What kind of husband do you think I am?"

"We're not married."

"The clerk thinks we are."

"Be serious, Chip."

"I am." He stopped and turned her to face him squarely. "I'm not sugar-coating how I feel, Angela. I've never been so in love in my life. Do you think I'd walk out now, and never see you again?"

Angela was surprised at the seriousness in his tone. A frown creased his lovely, high forehead and his eyes narrowed. "Is that what you were going to do?"

"Well, I—"

He gathered her in his arms and held her tightly.

"Angela, you may think I have air for brains, but I've had a feeling about you since you saved my hide two weeks ago. I've dreamed about you—wondered about you—and when you stepped onto my plane that day . . . I knew we'd be together."

The young woman felt her heart soar. What he was saying was crazy, but if there was such a thing as fate, maybe this was it. In all her twenty-eight years, she'd never become so blinded by feelings she couldn't deny. Men had come and gone in her life, but she didn't dare dream that this one would love her as he claimed. Maybe they could arrange their lives to accommodate a long-distance relationship . . . he in California and she in Colorado. Traveling wouldn't be a problem for either of them, since they both had access to free airfares, but their schedules could be trouble.

"And, Miss Lawrey," he said, wrapping his arms around her. "I'm old-fashioned enough to believe that someday you'll be my bride."

"Aren't you rushing things a bit?" Angela asked.

"I've waited almost twenty years to meet you."

"I don't know you at all."

"Sure you do. I told you all about my brilliant past as a naval fighter pilot. I told you how I started with Westair five years ago. You know all about my son. And I know everything about you that I need to know." He finished with a wicked grin.

"Like what?"

"You look like an angel and have the brains of a tactical genius. What else do I need to know?"

"You don't even know my full name," she accused.

"Yes I do. It's Angel Lawrey."

"Angela Germaine," she corrected.

"You don't snore—"

"I don't cook."

"You won't have to," Chip said, squeezing her lightly. "We'll eat out a lot."

"I won't give up my job."

"I wouldn't want you to."

"No?" she asked, her eyebrow raising in disbelief.

"Why? Did you want me to give up mine?"

"Of course not," she chided. "It's just that most men think the woman's career is second to theirs. Kids and housekeeping come first."

"Not in my book," Chip defended. "I've got a full-grown son, and I don't plan to start another family this late in the game."

"Oh." Angela thought her voice sounded small and far away. Chip wasn't going to make demands on her that others had. For that she was relieved and grateful—and at a loss for words. Every argument she presented he had countered. But what he was proposing was absurd. Wasn't it?

"People just don't meet and fall in love like this, Chip. You're not serious, are you?"

He looked crestfallen. "Honey, I wouldn't have believed it myself six months ago. But unless you've got a deep dark secret that I need to know about, there's no use arguing. I'm in love with you." He kissed her lightly, and they headed down the narrow, two-lane street, arm in arm.

They spent the afternoon browsing local shops where Angela purchased a string bikini and a few trinkets as souvenirs. Chip checked out the fishing gear in a sports and dive shop, and settled for a new lure he could try out on the pier.

Angela was surprised to discover that Chip knew the storeowner, Sammy Nakata, on a first-name basis. She had blushed when Chip introduced her to Sammy as "the love of his life."

She caught herself daydreaming about how life would be if she were married to the charismatic pilot. She'd be the envy of female Westair employees, that was a given. What she didn't know was how she'd handle being the wife of this Texas-bred romantic.

"Angela, where would you like to go for dinner tonight?" Chip's cheerful voice broke into her thoughts and instantly brought her back to the present.

"I like Japanese."

"Then you'll like this place. Come on. Let's rest up a bit, change, then I'll take you to *Kyoto Gardens*."

She had given Chip the key when they left for lunch, so this time he unlocked the door, and with a gallant flourish swept her off her feet and carried her across the hotel room threshold.

"Chip," Angela squealed as he lifted her off her feet.

"Welcome home, darlin'." He set her down at the foot of the bed.

"You're so—so—"

"I keep telling you, there aren't and won't be any other ladies in my life. I'm yours for keeps. You rest up now, while I take care of reservations and reacquaint myself with the town. I'll be back in a while."

Angela felt relaxed and free of worry as she pulled the soft sheet over her shoulder. It was truly as if they'd known each other for years, and were rediscovering the love they had waited for. She sighed deeply and fell into a dream.

Angela's voice was clear and confident as she directed the planes to DIA Air Tower. The blips on her screen seemed to multiply as she watched them coming in from all directions, converging in chaos. Suddenly all the planes disappeared as Chip's voice broke the air.

"Westair 143 to DIA tower. Do you copy?"

Angela tried to make contact, but her equipment seemed to have failed.

"Do you copy?" Captain Stephens repeated.

"I hear you. Can you read me?"

"DIA Tower, do you copy?"

Another plane entered the landing pattern and began circling. "Denver tower this is Eastways 267 requesting permission to land."

"267 this is Denver Tower. Over." Angela shouted, trying to be heard.

"Denver tower, flight 267 requesting permission to land."

Angela's hands began to sweat as the tempo of her heart accelerated. She felt her throat tighten as if the air in the room was smothering her. Her voice lost volume and she rasped, "Richie, they don't hear me. I can't get through." Richie's face grew pale as he studied the radar screen. In horror, they realized the two giant aircraft were on a deadly course. "They're too close, they won't make it! What can I do?"

"You've got to handle it, Ang. You're the pro."

Angela watched, aghast, as Richie stood up and walked away. "Richie, don't leave. Come back here," she wailed. "Richie!"

Her station began to rock and the room tilted. Everything went black. "Richie!"

"Angel. Wake up, darlin'. Angela." Chip leaned over the sleeping woman, shaking her. "Angela—"

Her heart pounded as if she'd been running. Perspiration swathed her body and the sheet had tangled around her. She blinked her eyes open and became aware of Chip.

"Oh, Chip. I'm so sorry. I don't know what's come over me."

"Are you all right?"

"Yes." She tugged the sheet loose, sat upright, then wedged it beneath her arms. "What a dream! Horrible."

Chip tenderly swept a tangled strand of hair away from her face. "You've been away a couple of days. It's not unusual to worry about work when you're gone."

It embarrassed her that Chip had witnessed this deviation in her behavior. She felt weak and stupid. How much of her dream had she shouted? *He must think I'm cracking from the stress.*

"What did I say?" she muttered dejectedly.

"You kept calling Richie."

"My partner."

Chip's face tightened. "Is he—"

Reading his thoughts, Angela answered sternly, "He's my data position partner. That's all. But I felt like he walked out on me. I was having this weird dream, and you were in it too."

"It'd have to be weird if I was in it," he chuckled.

"It didn't make sense. Everything was crazy and no one could hear me."

"It didn't mean anything, then, if it was all jumbled up like that."

"I must look awful," she said shaking her unruly head of hair.

"You look beautiful." Combing her hair tenderly with his fingers, he asked, "Feeling better?"

"Yes." This time she meant it.

Kyoto Gardens was a world of difference from *Shanty Jack's* dive. Colorful paper lanterns lit their way as they walked through a meticulously landscaped Japanese garden of bamboo plants. They passed giant goldfish ponds lined with lava rocks, and over an arched bridge. The restaurant was a replica of a true Japanese home, built with cherry wood and opaque paper walls and windows. A Japanese woman dressed in a traditional kimono greeted them at the door with a low bow. After Chip and Angela removed their shoes, the woman provided them with cotton foot coverings.

They followed her into a partitioned room. A hibachi and low table were positioned in the center, surrounded by cushions. Rieko was their hostess for the evening, and she remained with them throughout the meal. The tea service was delicate hand-painted white china depicting an ibis in flight. The screen separating their room had a watercolor painting of Mt. Fuji with a mountain waterfall pouring into a stream. A lilting flute provided the mesmerizing music that helped send them into another realm. Chip caught Angela's gaze several times during the meal as they enjoyed sushi, miso and a variety of tempura vegetables. The look on his face was the look of pure love.

It fascinated him that a creature as feminine and beautiful as Angela was also so independent and as tough as nails when it came to her job. She had to be. But she carried it off without losing the mysterious allure that was natural to a woman.

Her floral perfume reminded him of the afternoon she had entered the plane. He had assumed the woman was the stewardess, but how fortunate for him it had been Angela. His life had certainly changed since that meeting. He was enraptured with her. She was indeed his angel. Angela wore an emerald green sarong that circled her neck. He whistled softly. "Good thing they keep the lights down," he said, sliding his finger along the soft material around her neck.

Her hands slipped around his waist.

Chip flicked at her layered silver earrings that jingled softly. Her eyes were a deep green velvet that fixed lovingly on his face. She had swept her hair off one ear and secured it with a tortoiseshell comb, letting the rest fall loose and casual.

"You're beautiful, Angela. How did I get so lucky?"

"I was wondering how *I* got so lucky."

Angela felt pampered and relaxed and totally removed from the real world. The evening had been completely captivating, ever since they left the entrance gate and walked through time to enter the sliding door of Kyoto. When they returned to the hotel that night, she felt as if she walked on air, with Chip at her side. Sleepily, she leaned against him as they strolled through the spacious lobby. Except for the desk clerk, it seemed everyone else had turned in for the night.

Angela stretched and yawned. She couldn't remember when she had slept so well.

Chip turned from his view at the window when he heard her stirring. He sat on the edge of her bed and combed her hair with the tenderness of his tapered fingers. "Morning, Angel."

"What time is it?"

"The fish quit bitin' about two hours ago."

"You've been out already?"

"Yep."

"I've slept through two days of my vacation," she complained. "If I don't get some sunshine, no one will believe I ever left this hotel room."

"That's what I was thinking," Chip agreed. "I ordered brunch to be served on the patio. How's that sound?"

"You're so thoughtful. Is there anything you *don't* do right?"

He chuckled and his eyes sparkled like sunlight dancing on water. "No one's perfect, Angela, but I aim to please."

"I think you hit the target, Stephens." Angela pulled the covers aside and swung her legs over the edge of the bed.

Chip opened his arms to her and hugged her. "My mama always said, 'When you find a good woman you better treat her like a queen'."

"I think I like your mother." Angela grinned.

"I know you will."

Slipping from his grasp, she changed the subject. "I believe I'll try out that new bikini today,"

"You're not going to wear that little string thing on the beach, are you?"

"That's what I bought it for. Do you object?" she teased.

"Not at all."

They walked hand-in-hand to the beach. While Angela

sunbathed on the full-size towel, Chip plodded through the sand toward the pier to try out his new lure.

Angela shaded her eyes and watched as he grew smaller in the distance. It had been an incredible two days together. She would miss him terribly. After today they only had one more day, and then they'd both be back at work. His in the air, hers on the ground.

She shifted her body and smoothed out a lump of sand to accommodate her shoulders. "Live for today," she mumbled. *And cry tomorrow,* she thought sadly.

Chip gazed at the reclining beauty who lay tanning in the sun. Just the sight of her made him feel good. Her laughter drifted into his thoughts, along with the floral scent of the island flowers that lined the nearby park. He hadn't regretted taking the unplanned leave for a moment since he'd joined Angela on Kauai. In fact, it had been the most brilliant thing he'd done lately. What was he going to do now, though? She lived somewhere in Colorado, and he was based in Los Angeles. Unless someone was planning to transfer or retire from Westair in Denver, he couldn't make a move. Angela had told him she wasn't ready to get married. She needed time to adjust to having a man in her life—one who didn't make unfair demands on her or her time. She was everything he had dreamed of in a mate— but maybe she wasn't sure he was right for her. *I can't rush her anymore than I already have. Just bide your time, Stephens. It'll work out,* he told himself.

"Hey, buddy." An old-timer pointed to Chip's fishing pole as it dipped and bobbed.

"Whoa," Chip shouted, pulling up his line. "Looks like I got something."

Chip had an audience as he reeled it in. After he disengaged a brightly-colored fish, he handed it over to the man and secured his line.

"Time to go." Chip smiled at the old man as he left the pier. Things would work out between himself and Angela Germaine Lawrey. He was sure of it.

Chapter Four

Monday morning came too quickly. Angela awoke in her Longmont condominium to a chiming that grew progressively louder as she ignored the initial tones. She reached beside her to quiet the alarm and raised her eyes to the ceiling. Just three days ago she lay in a double bed with nothing but a sheet hanging between her and the very attractive Chip Stephens. *Where is he this morning?*

Angela sat up and gradually collected her thoughts. She would have a report to file in addition to her regular duties today. And the day was at hand. She opened the blinds in the living room and looked out. The morning sun painted the mountains in delicate watercolor shades of pink and violet. The sky was robin-egg blue without a trace of clouds. She never failed to stop and take in that morning view, since it was the last she would see of the mountains until the end of the day.

Quickly she showered, dressed and ate a light breakfast. As she downed the last of her orange juice, she recalled the brunch Chip had delivered on their balcony. They had fresh-squeezed juice, crumpets and Hawaiian coffee. From their perch, they watched the ocean wash against the shore and laughed at the seagulls that danced out of the way. It had been a wonderful four days. But when Chip left her at the airport it had ended. For the first time in her life, Angela understood the word *lonely*.

She looked around her kitchen and, confident that all was in order, locked the door and left.

A few minutes later, she waited behind a string of cars until the Denver Center gate guard waved her through. She was one of the first morning-shift personnel in the parking lot that Monday as she eased her convertible into a space and locked it. Focused on her job, she marched into the building and the heavy door closed daylight behind her.

Inside the crew's lounge she spied her partner. "Hey, Richie—how's Longmont's most eligible?"

"What d'ya say, An-gee? How was Hawaii?"

"Not bad. Charming company. Nice hotel. Lots of beach."

"Charming company?" Richie leaned into Angela's shoulder. "Meet someone interesting?"

"Maybe." She smiled.

"Mr. Right?" He twisted his face into a comical mask. "Big island man—got plenty coconuts?"

Angela laughed. "Close, but not quite. So, Richie . . . catch me up. What's been going on since I've been gone?"

Richie instantly sobered. "Actually a lot has happened. We're still reeling."

"Really? What happened?"

"The National Airspace System was non-operational for three days. We had to use the backup system."

"The DARC?" Angela asked, shocked.

"You got it. The Direct Access Radar Channel. It causes more fatigue and stress, and you know how the union hates that."

"Increases risk of human failure," Richie and Angela chanted in unison, as if they'd heard that litany a hundred times.

"Oh, brother. I can't believe the NAS was down. I'm glad I was gone. What about the other radar sites? Were they having trouble also?"

"North Platte, Nebraska went down when we were on DARC, so the adjacent site had to cover four or five sectors. Here, look at this."

Richie produced headlines from the local paper that had picked up the story.

"Geez. Can't we keep something like this out of the news? This is enough to scare people half to death."

"And drop pleasure flights significantly if the paper can be believed," Richie added.

Angela read further. "Near miss? Westair and a private craft? They're talking about me!"

"It gets worse."

Two aircraft flew too close to each other and remained unreported although a collision was imminent. An unnamed female controller conducting personal conversation over the air failed to notice a private craft in commercial jet space.

"This is unbelievable." Angela breathed a heavy sigh. "And I thought I missed this place."

"There's plenty of heat on, but it looks like you're the only one who managed to get a tan."

Angela inspected her skin tone, rubbing her hand lightly over her arm. "Barely."

At that moment Bob Haskell arrived. "Lawrey, come into my office for a moment. Are you free?"

"Right away," she answered. When Haskell retreated, Angela whispered, "How're the rest of the crew doing?"

"Morale is about as low as whale feed and that's—"

"At the bottom of the ocean," Angela finished. "Gotcha."

"Hang in there, Ace."

"Thanks, Richie." She patted her partner's shoulder as she turned and left the room.

Angela stepped into Haskell's office. The south-facing window allowed a view of the housing development that had grown up where cornfields once stood. The room was bright in contrast to the darkened atmosphere of the control room.

"Come in, Lawrey. Take a seat." Haskell tilted his executive chair back and eyed his visitor. "How was your trip?"

Angela felt her stomach quiver slightly. "Fine. Good ride both ways."

"Filed your debrief report yet?"

"In the box this morning."

"Good. Good."

"I hear we had a problem with the primary computer again," she ventured.

"Yes. We identified the problem, but it took almost three days to correct." His chair tilted forward. "But that's not what I wanted to talk about, and that's not why I called you in."

"I saw the article," she said.

Haskell folded his fingers and leaned his chin on his upraised thumbs. "A little inaccurate, isn't it?"

"Is this a formal counseling session?" Angela felt the hair on the back of her neck bristle. "Am I under suspicion of wrong-doing?"

"Of course not. I just want your side of the story in case this goes any further."

"I wasn't conducting a personal conversation." Angela assessed her supervisor. "I directed the pilot away before—" she felt her face redden as she remembered the aftermath.

"Yes?"

"I gave the pilot my call sign."

"He asked for it?"

"Yes. I guess that's how—"

"No matter, Lawrey. It's done. Could be that Westair letter of appreciation generated some jealousy, although I can't believe a professional would deny you that. You averted a collision, for God's sake. It's not like you were discussing dinner and a date, right?"

Haskell is treading too close to the truth. Feeling uncomfortable, Angela shifted in her seat. "The computer? Is everything back on line?"

"We initialized a fail-safe backup that should take care of any recurrence. It was a freak. With as many flights as we have a day, we can't afford a repeat. I remember back in '68 when I was a rookie at the New York Center, everyone got a twenty dollar bonus for working four thousand flight operations in one day."

"With the equipment you had back then, that quota would have been phenomenal."

"Yeah, but as busy as you people are—close to six thousand—you're busting backs about as much as we did."

Angela studied the serious face of the man in front of her.

"Lawrey, I don't need to tell you that, because you're

one of the new breed around here. You're under extraordinary pressure."

"Because I'm the new guy on the block?"

"And you're a top performer, and you're young, and—"

"I'm a woman," she sensed his hesitation.

"I wasn't going to say that."

"You didn't have to."

"From all the reports I've seen—and I've had to monitor them all—" he added. "You've got a good shot at area supervisor."

Angela didn't attempt to conceal her pleasure at his suggestion. She smiled.

"Now don't get premature on me," Haskell cautioned her. "You've got a long way to go yet. There are more snags and snares and hurdles to cross—"

"Are you trying to scare me, Bob, or is this your idea of a motivational speech?"

"I just want you to know that not everybody is on your side. I am, but I'm only one person."

"I understand."

"You're going to have to be better than anyone else."

Angela nodded. "Just for the record, who's my competition?"

"Sam Rankin, for one."

"He's a fifteen-year veteran. I'm up against him?"

"He's been in line for promotion for some time, but you've got a good shot at it."

"I don't think he likes me."

"You upstarts are a threat to the old guard. You know that. But just so you know . . . everyone is being closely monitored. We don't know who leaked the news about some of these sensitive situations, but this doesn't look good for us or the FAA in general."

Angela considered that information.

"And another thing, Lawrey . . ."

Angela smiled sweetly. "What's that?" She watched his neck deepen a shade of pink that she recognized when he became nervous.

"Your character and off-duty associations have got to be above reproach. I don't want anyone sneaking behind your back and then tattling in here that you're soiling your good name—along with your chance for advancement."

It was Angela's turn to color. She felt the familiar blush flame her cheeks and ears. Tilting her head she narrowed her gaze, locking onto Bob's face. "Excuse me?"

"I didn't say it's come up, Lawrey, I'm just trying to forewarn you."

Angela stood suddenly. "I assure you, Mr. Haskell, my behavior thus far has been and will remain impeccable. I don't intend to jeopardize my career—my livelihood. You won't need to bring it up again."

"Now don't get on your high horse, Lawrey. You know I think of you like I would my own daughter, and I want to see you promoted almost as much as you do. Just remember I'm here, and if you need anything, you come to me first. You got it?"

"Yes, sir," she responded stiffly.

"Good." He planted his hands on the upholstered arms of his oversized chair. "Good," he repeated. "I'll look over that report later today."

"Would that be all?"

"Yes. Thanks for coming in."

The young woman turned to leave.

"Angela?" Haskell stopped her. "Don't forget, I'm on your side."

Sighing, Angela nodded. "I know, Bob. Thanks."

Richie was at their station when Angela returned. It was not until their lunch break that they had a chance to visit again. Instead of leaving for lunch, Angela went to the cafeteria with Richie.

Richie piled his plate with potato salad, beans and a Rueben sandwich. "What did Haskell have to say?"

"He told me to watch my step. We're all being monitored. Did you know that?"

"Kinda," he admitted. "Same old stuff, you know."

Angela picked at her salad and speared a slice of cucumber. "I don't like having to worry about people looking over my shoulder. It's like being back at training. I had enough of that at the Aeronautical Center in Oklahoma. I thought I had graduated," she groused.

"Welcome to the real world. Jungle tactics 101."

"It doesn't bother you?"

"Nah. As long as you're doing your job, you'll be all right. You're the pro, Ang. But I will tell you this." He leaned toward her and lowered his voice. "Don't trust anyone, Angela. Not even Haskell."

"But he's my supervisor."

"We're all under scrutiny. Even Haskell. Do you think if things got bad, he'd risk his neck to save yours?"

Angela cocked her head and thought about it. *Richie might be right.* She looked at her partner, his boyish features honest and unmasked. *He is probably right.*

Richie took the last bite of his giant sandwich.

"What about—"

"Believe me," he interrupted, reading her thoughts. "No one."

*   *   *

The phone stopped ringing just as Angela unlatched the deadbolt and pushed open the heavy, carved door to her condominium. She heard the answering machine pick up and a man's voice come over the speaker. "Angela, honey, this is Chip. Just checkin' in to see how you fared on your first day back to work. I've got to run, so I'll call you later this week. My number is—" Her antiquated system cut him off before he could leave a number. Angela punched the button to silence the machine and picked up the receiver then set it down. Chip had been disconnected.

"Me and my old-fashioned gadgets," she scolded herself. "Someday—"

The phone rang again. Angela picked up the handset before it rang a second time.

"Chip?"

"Hi, honey. How'd you know it was me?"

"I just walked in." She felt a girlish tingle rising in her throat. "I'm sorry the machine cut you off."

"That's okay. How're you doing?"

Angela felt as if she'd been driving a big rig all day. The stress and aggravations had her muscles knotted tight. All those feelings dissipated, though, as she focused on the man's voice. "I'm good. Where are you?"

"I'm in between flights. Had a layover in Houston, so I thought I'd give you a call. You made it back, I see."

Angela perched on an antique hall chair and twirled the twisted cord around her index finger. "Yes. You too? How have you been?"

"You'd have to compare me to a lovesick calf, moping around like I am. The fellas are getting a kick out of me," he confessed.

"Chip Stephens, you're impossible. One date with a girl and you'd think I hung the moon."

"You have, if anyone asks me. I miss you, darlin'."

Angela smiled at his admission. "We had fun, didn't we?"

"I don't know about you, but I thought I'd died and gone to heaven."

"It's nice of you to call, Chip."

"I told you I would. When am I going to see you again?"

"I live in Colorado."

"I'll be in this week. How about Saturday? Are you busy?"

"It's probably not a good idea, Chip. I haven't even been home a week and I have lots—"

"I'd sure like to see you again."

"Me too," she admitted.

"What if I layover Saturday?"

Bob Haskell's conversation blitzed through Angela's thoughts. "I don't know, Chip. I'd like to, but—"

"You think about it, I don't want to trouble you with it right now. Oh, I almost forgot. Let me give you my number."

Angela reached for a pad and pen near the telephone and took his phone number.

"I'll call you back Thursday, Angel. I've gotta go."

Angela listened until the dial tone indicated the line was dead. "Darn." *Why didn't I just say yes? What am I afraid of? Haskell? The press?* She replaced the handset on the receiver and stepped down into the sunken area of the cool, expansive living room, kicking off her shoes as she descended. Floor-to-ceiling vertical blinds opened up to an unobstructed view of Mt. Meeker and Longs Peak. The afternoon sun lightened the Colorado sky and tinted the puffy cumulous clouds into shades of gold, orange and pink. *What can I be thinking of?* She argued with herself. *Am I crazy? I couldn't think of leaving Colorado and he lives in Los Angeles. It is impossible.*

Chapter Five

After Angela arrived home from work on Thursday, she answered the doorbell to a floral deliveryman.

"Miss Angela Lawrey?"

"Yes?"

"These are for you." Handing an exotic floral bouquet to her, the young man continued, "This is a special delivery order from our Denver location."

Angela accepted the vase, admiring the exotic flowers. She recognized several of the blossoms as those from Hawaii. She thanked him, closed the door and set the arrangement in her living room.

The card that accompanied the gift read, *To My Angel, with love, Chip.*

She smiled, pleased that Captain Stephens evidently intended to keep his word. This Texas-raised pilot seemed determined to "rope" her into his life. And to date, he was scoring pretty well. Angela bent to smell the brightly colored arrangement, and the scent took her back to balmy nights in Kauai. For a moment, she let her mind wander to the waves that gently broke on the shore and raced back again in their endless advance and retreat. She inhaled the sweet fragrance again. Angela placed the card beside the vase and wished he were here. For now, the flowers would have to do in his stead.

After a vigorous workout at the pool, Angela returned home, punched the playback button on her answering machine and turned up the volume. The device rattled as it reversed, stopped, clicked and began playing her phone messages. Angela listened from the kitchen as she prepared a light meal. There was a message from a long-distance telephone service, and another one from Chip. She stopped when she heard his voice. "Hi darlin', just wanted to check in with you and see if Saturday is an option. My flight terminates at DIA 4:30 Saturday. I'll be flying out of Denver Sunday morning. I'll call tomorrow unless you want to leave a message—"

The machine cut him off. Angela bee-lined for the answering machine, punched the rewind button and heard the old machine straining to rewind. "Darn machine. Keep it up and I'll replace you someday."

After she had eaten and cleaned the kitchen she returned her calls. Chip's voice mail prompted her to leave a message, and Angela told him Saturday was free and clear.

Chip arrived shortly after six P.M. in a rented car. Still wearing his Westair uniform, he looked like a military officer when she opened her door to him. Removing his flat-top hat at the door with the grace and ease of years of practice, Captain Stephens stepped inside.

Angela was surprised at the nervous fluttering in her stomach. Chip circled his arms around her and gathered her close before kissing her lightly. The spaghetti strap on her pale yellow sundress fell from her shoulder. He lifted the thin strap with one finger, and drew it back onto her shoulder, trailing an electric tingling that caused her to shiver.

"Boy, I've missed you." He whistled softly.

"You remember this dress? I wore it on the island." Angela felt herself blushing like a teenager.

"Seems like a month ago."

"It's hardly been a week," she reminded him.

"You look better than I remembered."

She smiled. "Don't embarrass me, now. You haven't even gotten in the door and you're flattering me. Come in. Do you want to change?"

"I have a bag in the car. I thought if you didn't mind, I'd take you out to dinner. Do you have plans?"

"Only to spend time with you. I told you Saturday was clear."

"Good." Captain Stephens looked pleased. "Where shall we go?"

"We could drive up to Estes Park if you'd like. It's a nice drive, and not too far away. I'll drive."

"Sounds great. I'll be just a minute."

Stephens gathered his things and came back in.

"The guest room's on the left." Angela directed him.

"You've got a nice place here, Angel."

"Thanks. I like it."

Chip changed quickly and reemerged wearing casual pants and a knit shirt that would have been suitable for a golf course or a casual dinner. "How's this?" he asked.

"You look nice."

"I'm in good company then." He smiled. "Where are we going?"

"I have a place in mind called Baron's. It's on the west end of Estes."

Stephens followed her into her enclosed garage. Inside sat her gold-colored convertible.

"Whewee, baby." He whistled. "Nice ride. 450?"

"350 SL. You're impressed?" she teased.

"Fancy lady, fancy wheels. I must say, I know how to pick 'em."

Angela pressed the automatic door opener and the afternoon light flooded in.

"Hop in. It's open."

She slid into the driver's side, stuck the key into the ignition, and started the engine. A muffled "varooom" emitted from the stately two-passenger sedan as Captain Stephens joined her in the small cockpit. In a few short minutes they left Longmont and were headed west into the mountains.

"I'll take you the long way around, so you can see more of the scenery. You haven't been up here before, have you?"

"Never. Can't say I've ever been outside DIA, as far as Colorado goes."

"You're missing a lot, then. This is the most beautiful country I've ever seen."

She drove through the sleepy main street of Lyons, then turned left at the "T" in the road. A clear mountain stream bordered the road on the left, winding its way east toward the prairies of eastern Colorado. As they climbed higher into the mountains, the stream bed became narrower, forcing the water through natural rock chutes into waterfalls and boulder-rife channels.

"This is the South St. Vrain River," Angela explained. "Named after a French fur trapper in the area."

"Back home we call something like this a 'spit ditch.' "
Chip smiled. "But few people understand that this is where
it all starts—out of the mountains at the Continental Divide.
I'll bet there's fly-fishing in that stream."

They drove past homesteads that looked as if they'd
stood since the late eighteen hundreds, and left the lower
valley by way of a curving mountain road that allowed
views of several mountain ranges.

"This is a nice road for a car like this. It drives so
smoothly and really hugs those corners." Chip patted her
hand. "You're a good driver."

"Coming from a man who flies jumbo jets, I'll consider
that a compliment, Captain."

As they crested the top of a hill, an awesome view of a
snow-laden mountain dominated the panorama. An obvious
"V" crevice filled with snow marked its otherwise smooth
eastern face. "Mount Meeker," she announced. "Isn't it
beautiful?"

"I'll say. We don't have anything like *that* back home."

"That's the mountain you can see from my living room.
From this angle, though, it's hiding Long's Peak. We'll see
that just down the road."

"There's still a lot of snow up there."

"I'm told the farmers can gauge the ditch water based
on how much snow is left in that crevice by the fourth of
July."

"Looks like they'll do all right this year." Chip guessed.

The road circled in front of the peak into yet another
forested area, then passed another meadow. On the left, Mt.
Meeker rose massive behind a lovely stone chapel that
seemed to have grown straight out of the rocks.

"Let's stop here for a moment, can we?" Chip asked

"Sure. It is pretty, isn't it?" Angela wheeled the car off

the road into the parking lot at the base of the chapel. Together they walked around the rocks on a path that took them through the willows, then opened up above a beaver-made moat. The church's reflection and images of clouds shimmered in the little pond.

Looking west toward the mountains, Meeker was the perfect backdrop to the little stone chapel. The scene could have been two thousand years old, and transported from high in the European Alps.

"I thought you'd like this route," Angela whispered. "It's not as heavily traveled as the North St. Vrain Canyon.

"It's perfect, honey. I can't say I've ever seen anything so peaceful, so beautiful." He held her hand as they walked back to the car. "Thank you for bringing me here." He squeezed her gently, then opened her door and closed it behind her.

They continued their drive past Lily Lake. They saw another perfect view of the town of Estes Park as they maneuvered the narrow mountain road, high on the cliffs above the valley. Dusk transformed the sky from daylight into muted hues of blue-tinted clouds, edged in gold from lingering sunlight. Soon the mountains shadowed the valley in a sleepy blanket of darkness.

"My goodness, this is pretty country. No wonder you like it here."

"I love it," Angela corrected. "I don't plan to ever leave."

"I can sure see why. It's beautiful, darlin'."

Angela drove through the tourist-crowded streets of Estes Park, then wheeled in front of Baron's, an upscale restaurant, by the look of it, on the west end of town. When they stepped inside, again they were transported into old Europe. Dark wooden walls, brass and crystal chandeliers,

Louis XIV chairs, and an antique wall tapestry graced the dining area.

The hostess seated them near a glass wall that over-looked the stream. After some discussion, Chip ordered two glasses of champagne. Raising his glass to his companion, Chip said, "To the woman who saved my life—not once, but twice—Angela, I salute you."

Angela smiled, feeling a blush fan her cheeks. "It was luck, Captain Stephens, the first time. How do you figure a second?"

"The day you stepped onto my flight and I met you in person, you made me realize how lucky I was to be alive, and that I might truly love again."

Angela studied the seriousness in his blue eyes. She had seen the playful, boyish side of him, as well as the quiet and introspective side. At this moment she witnessed the solemnity of a man of a serious nature, profound and sin-cere. She believed she could love for the first time.

Dinner at Baron's was a two-hour affair that began with hors d' oeuvre then progressed with whole grain rolls, soup, salad, and eventually the entree. Over dinner, Angela talked about her family and the Nebraska home where she was raised. The only child of a mid-western couple, she had the personality and firmness inherited from her father, and the high-mindedness and culture learned from her mother. Chip admired her mix of softness and strength.

After the dishes had been cleared and coffee served, Chip reached across the table and covered her hands with his. "I'd like to show you Texas, Angel. I want you to see where I came from. Would you consider coming to the ranch and meeting my folks?"

"Well, sure, but—"

"It wouldn't cost you a thing. I'll take care of all of the arrangements."

"I just got back, you know. I'd have to check my calendar."

"Of course. With any luck our schedules might coordinate."

"I think I have a three-day break coming up," she said.

"That would be perfect. I could take you around San Antonio, the Alamo—"

"I thought we were going to your ranch?"

"We'll work that in too. Say yes," he coaxed. "It'd be a nice break for you. My folks would love the company."

"You're very persuasive, Captain. Do you ever take no for an answer?"

"You wouldn't want to break a poor boy's heart, would you?"

"Of course I'll go. When I get back to work I'll check the assignments."

"It'll be my turn to guide you around some beautiful country. You won't regret it."

As they left the restaurant, Chip draped his arm about her shoulder. Angela liked the lights in Captain Stephens' eyes, full of life and fun. *How could I refuse anything he suggested?*

Rainbow-colored shafts of light painted the twin lakes that bordered the road out of town. Through Ponderosa pine forests, they wound through the canyon until it opened up into a meadow. Her high beams caught the reflection of large animals standing alongside the road.

"Look, Chip. Elk!" Angela pointed. A big bull elk stood proud, guarding his charges. Small nubs of horns were in evidence. The meadow was covered with elk of varying sizes.

She slowed the car and eased onto the shoulder of the road. The elk, grazing on tender grasses, seemed to ignore them. "They're not skittish like deer," Angela explained.

"They are big, aren't they?"

"Hungry too. They usually start calving in May."

"They look pretty healthy," Chip noted. "Must not have had too hard a winter."

"Our winters are usually pretty mild, believe it or not." Angela watched the bull raise and lower his head. "People have an exaggerated opinion of Colorado's snowfall. It's never been as bad as Nebraska," she added.

"I've never lived where it snowed to any degree. I think we had two inches once, about sixteen years ago. Bobby Ray liked it, but it didn't last long. Not enough to try sledding or anything."

Angela started the engine, and they continued down the canyon on the curving mountain road. Several clusters of homes dotted the forest that bordered them on both sides. Darkness overtook the landscape where no buildings stood. Eventually they reached the settlement of Pinewood Springs, following a gradual rise to the crest of the hill. On the top of the ridge, the lights of Denver and the valley in between radiated heavenward.

"Pull over here," Chip coaxed. "I'd like to see this."

Angela edged the car to the side of the road beneath a tall pine and cut the engine. For a moment they sat in silence as Chip surveyed his surroundings. Pine covered hills on both sides of the road opened up to the highway that wound down the mountain toward town. Star-like specks of commercial airliners blinked like fireflies.

"This would be a nice place for a house," Chip said. "You could look down into the valley and see the lights, but still be high enough to reach out and touch the stars."

"You're such a dreamer, Chip. You almost make me believe you would do it." In the muted green glow of the car's interior she watched the man beside her smile.

"Darlin', for you I'd fly to the moon."

Angela started her car. "You only have to come as far as Longmont to see me."

"Then you won't mind if I do?" He reached over and covered her hand with his warm grasp.

Angela eyed the man beside her. The small compartment seemed to have shrunk, and she was aware only of their breathing. "Anytime, Captain."

"I'll be back before you know it," he whispered.

"I'll count on that."

"We better get going. I have a long way to go tonight."

"You're not staying at my place?"

"No, Angel."

"But I have a guest room," she countered.

"I don't want to seem ungrateful, but it wouldn't do to have me leaving your home at first light. I made reservations in Denver before I left."

Angela understood. In view of the mood at Denver Center, he was right about appearances. Who knows how closely she was being monitored?

"That's considerate of you, Chip." She shifted into gear and began their descent down the mountain. "We'll be home in a few minutes."

They rode in silence, Chip studying their surroundings outside the car, Angela concentrating on the road ahead. Soon, she pulled into her garage.

Chip followed her inside and she dropped her purse onto the telephone chair by the front door.

"When will I see you again?" she asked.

"Soon as you tell me when you can take those three days. I'll meet you in Denver."

"I'll check the schedule at work and call you Monday."

Captain Stephens gathered her in his arms and held her for a moment. "Thanks for everything, Angel. I'll wait for your call."

When she closed the door behind him, Angela felt the emptiness swallow her. It would be a long time between his visits. Of that, she was sure.

Her schedule revealed a three-day break the last weekend in April. Angela left a message for Chip on Monday. She would see him again in less than two weeks, if his schedule was free.

The mood inside the Center was more tense than Angela had ever encountered. Another hostile media release had set management on edge.

"Isn't it enough that they exaggerate real situations?" she asked Richie. "Do they have to make up problems as they go along?"

"Don't know. Seems like they have more important issues to print, like how many loose dogs are in the city limits, and who didn't eradicate their dandelions. Important stuff like that."

Angela sighed. "I wish they'd find another bone to gnaw on for a while. Everyone seems so irritable." Angela looked around the lunchroom. "I've noticed more people are leaving at lunch time, just to get away."

"Yeah, I noticed that too. Say, are you going to finish your dessert or what?"

"No. You want it?" Richie snatched the cookie from her tray and wolfed them down before she had a chance to change her mind. "I guess you did. Were they good?"

"Um, hmm." He nodded.

"You're just like a teenager, Richie. It's a good thing you're here to keep my spirits up."

"Things could be worse."

"Yeah, I suppose."

"So what about this Prince Charming? You haven't mentioned him since you got back from Hawaii."

"Well . . ." She smiled, remembering her dinner with Chip last Saturday evening. "He's still in the picture."

"Does he live in Hawaii, or what?"

"Actually, remember the Westair pilot?"

"The one who asked you out?"

She glared at Richie.

"Sorry."

"Of all the planes that fly to L.A.—" she sighed.

"You're kidding?"

She shook her head.

"You met him?

"He followed me to Kauai."

"Whoa! Good work, Ang!"

"I won't see him again for a couple of weeks, though. He's taking me to meet his folks."

"So soon? You two must be serious."

"Well, I'm not ready to commit to a relationship. He knows that."

"So you're going steady, but not really?"

"I swear, Richie, you're about as nosey as my high school girlfriends."

"Sorry. I didn't mean to intrude."

She nudged his shoulder. "You're not. I guess I'm a little unsure of all this myself."

"He's not some kind of high-flying playboy, is he?"

"Hardly." Angela recalled the dividing sheet he had

strung between their beds at the Hanalei. "No. He's a country boy from Texas. Believes in a long courtship—an old-fashioned kind of guy."

Richie puffed up his chest, "Not too many of us left. Honorable. Handsome. Did I hear, rich?"

"He's a pilot, Richie. He works for a living just like we do."

"But if he's been flying for a while, he's probably worth a little. Sounds like a catch, Ang."

"You know very well I'm not looking for a bankroll. He's a nice guy and that's as far as it goes."

"Well, if he's as high-minded as you say he is, consider yourself fortunate. You'd go a long way to do better than that."

"Who says I'm looking to settle down at all," she countered. "Maybe I like the single life."

"It works for a while," Richie mused, "but cooking for one gets old."

Angela thought about Richie's comments. *Could be he's right about Captain Stephens. Maybe I should take him a little more seriously. But it would take time to get to know him—or anyone for that matter. And I don't have a lot of free time. My main concern is my career, and that should be enough for now.*

Chapter Six

As he had promised, Chip waited for Angela at the Westair ticket counter. He whistled softly as she approached.

"You are a sweet distraction, Ms. Lawrey. Did I tell you that you're the most beautiful woman on the planet?"

"Not this week." Angela smiled. "Are all you southern boys silver-tongued devils, or is that a Texas trait?"

Chip laughed. "I've never told a tale in my life." He kissed her on the cheek. "And I'm not about to start now."

He helped her check in with the Westair staff, then they waited in the officers' lounge. When their flight was called, Chip escorted her through the gangway and onto the aircraft. As they boarded, Chip stuck his head inside the cockpit.

"Hey guys—how's it goin'?"

"Not bad, buddy. What are you doing in civilian duds? A little R and R?"

"You could say that." Chip grinned.

Angela waited at Chip's side, but was noticed by the copilot.

"This your wife, Chip?"

"With any luck. Gentlemen, may I introduce you to Miss Angela Lawrey?" Chip stepped back, allowing Angela to move in front of him. She extended her hand to each as Chip introduced them, "Pete's the Captain, Rog Anderson, co-pilot and Tom Parry, navigator."

Tom studied her face for a moment. "Say, aren't you that controller?"

"That's right," Chip confirmed. "You were there when she came aboard that day."

"L.A. bound, right?" Tom recalled. "On your way to Maui, or—"

"Kauai," Angela corrected.

Tom swatted at Chip. "I thought you said the fishing wasn't that great in Kauai. Looks like you did all right."

"I wasn't fishing," Chip replied. "Come on, darlin'," Chip ushered Angela out of the cramped area. "We'll let these boys get back to work."

"Angela could take the jumpseat, Chip," the Captain volunteered.

"Not on this flight, guys, but thanks."

Angela heard them chuckling before the cockpit door clicked shut.

"I suppose you know all the pilots in your fleet?"

"Most of 'em. They're a pretty good bunch of guys."

"Any female pilots?"

"Three. They handle the coastal routes, mainly."

They settled into their assigned seats. Angela chose the window seat, Chip took the aisle.

"It's nice to have connections in the business," Angela

said, clamping on her seatbelt. "I'm not in the habit of flying somewhere on a whim."

"One of the benefits, darlin'. I wouldn't want any other kind of life."

After the plane left the concourse, the Captain welcomed the passengers and crew aboard. He announced that the flight was direct from DIA into San Antonio, and explained that they would be in the air about two and a half hours.

Following a light breakfast, Angela and Chip enjoyed their coffee at a cruising altitude of thirty one thousand feet. The weather forecast had predicted Texas would be enjoying highs in the seventies and lows in the fifties during their three-day visit.

"I'm sure glad you could afford the time off, Angel. This means a lot to me."

"Your parents are pretty generous to let you bring a stranger into their home. But knowing you, I'll bet this isn't a first."

"First for a female. I've had plenty of the guys over through the years. Little Bobby Ray was thrilled to have Dad's pals around. It's been a good arrangement for all of us. Bobby Ray's the rancher Pops always wanted. Don't get me wrong—I love the ranch and all, but I never wanted to be the ranchhand Pops was- -is, I should say. He'll be riding a horse when he's ninety, I suspect."

"So Bobby Ray—is he planning to go to college, or will he stay on the ranch after he graduates?"

"I've tried to talk him into Texas State, but I'm not sure. He's not too verbal when it comes to his plans."

"I bet he's had a difficult time, growing up without a mother."

"It wasn't easy, but we made the best of it. My mama is a saint. She and Bobby Ray are very close."

"Will I meet Bobby Ray, then?"

"I'm not sure, honey. I heard something about a school field trip. I didn't want him to change his plans."

"Of course not."

They traveled through partly cloudy skies above Abilene. "We're about an hour out of San Antonio," Chip guessed. "Not much longer."

"It's really not that far from Denver, is it?

"Just a hop, skip, and a jump," he said, patting her hand. "Are you nervous?"

"About the flight? No. Meeting your family? A little."

Chip laughed. "My mother's about as fearsome as a lamb, Angel. Pops . . . now he's a different story."

"Well, I hope they're not disappointed. But really, Chip, don't you think we're rushing things a bit? I mean, meeting your folks so soon. We're just dating, you know."

Chip pressed his hand to his heart in mock despair. "I'm wounded, Angel."

"Well, we *are* just dating. Long distance at that. This is the first time I've seen you in two weeks."

"Longest two weeks in history. If it weren't for the telephone lines, I would've been burning up the road between Denver and Longmont. But that's all going to change when you meet my folks. You'll fall in love with them, then you'll have to marry me."

Angela laughed. "One thing you certainly don't lack is charm, Captain Stephens."

He lifted her hand to his lips and kissed her fingers.

Two chimes over the intercom signaled the plane's descent. Angela peered out her window through cotton-candy puffs of clouds to the dense brushy hills below. "Lots of cumulus clouds over here. I love clouds."

"I suppose you had to learn all about that, didn't you?"

"It gave me an edge when I began training. I spent a lot of time as a youngster looking up at all the different faces and animals in those clouds. Then I got interested in learning about the weather. When I was in grade school, I thought about becoming a meteorologist."

"That's a pretty ambitious undertaking for a child," Chip remarked.

"My father thought so too. But being a farmer, he encouraged me to learn all I could about clouds. I became a sort of oddity, a pint-size farmer's almanac."

"He must have been proud of you."

"I suppose." She sighed. "Is this what you call 'hill country'?"

"Yep. I believe we're flying smack dab over the middle of it. Our ranch was under the flight path, and I'd stare up at the sky for hours watchin' those big jets fly by. Matter of fact, that's when I decided what I wanted to do. I'd look up at those planes wishing I was on them."

"How old were you?"

"I started that when I was about five years old. Old enough to wander down to the river by myself."

"Sounds like you were a bit of a prodigy yourself."

"Mama wouldn't say that. I'd tie a string onto a stick and go down to try to catch catfish or crawdads. Of course I didn't catch anything. She used to worry herself sick that I'd find a cottonmouth or drown in that little bit of water."

"Sounds like a typical mother."

"She had good reason come summertime. Our soil is pretty rocky, with lots of caliche and it gets so hard, it sets up like cement. When the rains come, the water doesn't have too many places to go. The Guadalupe flooded every year that I can remember."

"Really? It sounds dangerous."

"Only if you're caught in it. We have one high water bridge on our property—"

"Meaning?"

"Meaning it's the highest bridge from the river bottom, and if the water's running high, you better stay put."

"We won't need to be concerned about that this time of year, will we?"

"Nah. April is pretty calm. The wildflowers are about the roughest thing you'll encounter. You will have to mind the snakes, though."

"You're joking, I hope."

"Nope. Texas rattlers. Heads as big as my fist. You don't want to tango with one of them."

"I'll keep that in mind."

"Mama loves her wildflowers. They're real profuse down by the river in particular—primrose, blue bonnets, paintbrush. Even the weeds look pretty this time of year. Like I said before, Dad's still ranching a little, but not like the spread he used to have."

"Cattle?"

"White-faced Herefords. He thinks they've got the prettiest faces. He'd run as high as five hundred head when I was growin' up. He said he's got about a hundred now. A few horses, goats, chickens. It's a small ranch—two thousand acres."

"Two thousand! Chip, that's huge!"

"Not for running cattle, it isn't. You need about sixteen acres of undeveloped range to feed one steer. Dad cultivated about two hundred acres for grass hay. The rest he pretty much left to God's good hand."

"It sounds lovely."

"It is. We'll ride the fence line one afternoon so you can

get a good look. The South Fork of the Guadalupe runs through the lower part of the ranch."

"Where is it exactly? West of San Antonio?"

"Here, let me show you." Chip pulled the flight magazine from the pocket in front of him and flipped to the pages in the back. They should have a map of Texas in here." He located the flight chart and laid it on the arm rest between their seats. "See, here you can just about make out the Guadalupe. There's a little town called Ingram along the river. We're a few miles west and north of there—between Mountain Home and Ingram."

"We're getting in kind of early—are we going straight to the ranch?"

"I wanted to show you San Antonio this afternoon and evening, if you're not worn out. There are five different missions there, including the Alamo."

"I'd like to visit the Alamo. I also heard about some river walk area."

"Paseo del Rio. You'll love it. We'll have dinner along the River Walk. How does that sound?"

"Wonderful." Angela sighed. "You're spoiling me rotten, you know."

"That's my intention, Angel. This is my idea of a proper courtship."

After they had landed, Angela and Chip waited until all the other passengers had deplaned before they left their seats. They shook hands with Chip's associates and thanked them for the flawless ride.

"People sure are friendly in your company. Or is it just because of you?"

"Westair is terrific. I think most of the people I've met are of the same caliber. They're great people."

"You're not a little prejudiced, are you, Captain?"

"Maybe a little." He grinned. "Come on. Let's get our-
selves a car and get going."

Chip rented a Lincoln Towncar, with a champagne ex-
terior, pale leather upholstery and a CD player. "I'll give
you a tour of all the notable spots, Angel, and if there's
particular ones you'd like to visit, we'll stop. Let me know
if you want to take pictures, and I'll pull this baby over in
a heartbeat."

Angela laughed. "Okay, Chip. I'm happy with the view
for now. I need to get oriented a little."

He drove south on the freeway and pointed out the land-
marks. They headed toward the far end of San Antonio,
then Chip turned off the freeway and wound around a
poorer section of the city. He stopped in front of an old
mission. The sign in front proclaimed, *Mission San Jose y
San Miguel de Aguayo. Founded 1720.*

"This is one thing I wanted to show you, Angel."

Angela allowed Chip to open her door, and they walked
hand-in-hand through a rustic wooden gate into the courtyard. Angela eyed the lovely façade of the domed cathedral, admiring the skill with which it had been constructed.

"I don't suppose this mission was involved in the battles
around here?," she asked.

"No. But there's something here I wanted to show you."
Chip led her to the west side of the structure and pointed
out the beautifully scrolled design surrounding the window.
"This is what they call *Rosa's Window*. Legend has it when
the King of Spain sent this expedition to the Americas, he
ordered a particular carpenter to accompany them. He was
in love with a woman named Rosa, and they were engaged
to be married. He asked if Rosa could join him, but the
King denied his plea. He told the carpenter he would send
her to him as soon as he had finished his work. The work

took fourteen years. When he was through, the carpenter petitioned the King again to send Rosa. Word was sent back that Rosa had come some time prior, and apparently the ship had been lost at sea."

"Oh, that's tragic." Angela shook her head. "So sad."

"The man was so distraught, that he spent several years carving this beautiful sculpture in memoriam to his Rosa. He died here, and is buried in the mission cemetery."

"What a touching story."

"Yeah. I first heard that when I was a boy. Never forgot it."

They wandered the grounds around the cathedral and Chip pointed out the eighty individual "condos" the friars built for the Indians who numbered about four hundred at the time.

Angela watched, amused, as an arrogant-looking bird cackled and strutted the promenade in front of them. Its shiny feathers looked blue/black in the sunlight, and he appeared to be showing off.

"That's a great-tailed grackle," Chip explained. "They're about as noisy and proud a bird as they come."

"Must be Texan," Angela teased.

"Matter of fact, it is." Chip circled his arm around Angela. "Next stop San Antonio."

They drove north into the city and wound up in the downtown commercial section. He showed her the stately San Fernando Cathedral where Santa Anna's troops hung the red flag when they entered the city to retake the Alamo.

Chip swung the Towncar into the hotel's valet parking. He popped the trunk and pulled out their bags, and a uniformed bellboy loaded them onto a brass luggage gurney. The doorman assisted Angela from the Lincoln and she followed Chip inside the magnificent glass enclosed lobby.

"We'll be staying here tonight, and Saturday night at the ranch," Chip explained.

"Two rooms?"

"Yes, darlin'. This time we have *real* adjoining suites."

Angela smirked.

"I said I was a Boy Scout . . . not a saint."

They rode the glass elevator to the fourth floor. Below, Angela could see a decorative stream that coursed through the foyer from the canal. Tall exotic plants thrived in the glass-enclosed environment.

Angela followed the bellboy down the hall. He opened the door for her and carried her luggage inside. "Your room overlooks the River Walk, ma'am. Enjoy your stay."

Handing the young man a tip, Angela thanked him and strode across the luxurious carpet to the large bay window. A wall of windows overlooked the River Walk canal. San Antonio was a large, well-maintained city, rich in history, romantic and magical. To Angela, it seemed that Chip had arranged everything so perfectly, it would be impossible not to fall in love.

"It's beautiful, Chip."

"I don't think it has all the amenities of the Hanalei," Chip teased.

"You mean like rusty showerheads, and roosters that wake you in the morning?"

"You can't have everything, but I tried."

"This is so nice."

"You like it?" Chip stood behind her and gave her a little squeeze. "I hoped you would."

"It's lovely. Mind if I change before we go out?"

"Not at all. You call me when you're ready." Chip closed the door behind him.

Angela wandered again to the window that overlooked

the River Walk. Couples and families strolled the sidewalk that paralleled the canal. She watched, amused, as a boatload of tourists motored by. The guide, decked out like a Venetian boatman, manned a microphone and steered at the same time. It looked as if the passengers were enjoying themselves. She turned from the window and slipped off her shoes. This room was a far cry from the quaint, cramped room in the Hanalei that she and Chip had shared.

She felt a little overwhelmed by Chip's consistent sweetness and attentiveness. Although she enjoyed his company, and was certainly attracted to him, she wanted to pace the relationship a little more slowly than Chip, who expressed a desire for a serious and permanent involvement.

Angela changed, then rang his room.

"Ready to go?" Chip sounded eager. "I'll be right there."

They rode the elevator down to the canal level in the lobby, and Chip escorted her outside.

"It's so nice out." Angela breathed in the moist air. "It's humid, but not too bad."

"It's brutal in the summer, though. Dad's people headed for the hills when they first arrived in Texas."

"How long ago?" she asked.

"About a hundred years. 1869 as I recall."

"Oh, my, Chip. You didn't tell me your family homesteaded out here."

"I knew if you met my folks you'd hear it soon enough. Pops is third generation Texan."

"And your mother?"

"Mom's family moved in after it was a little more civilized—somewhere around the 1890's."

They followed the River Walk and headed toward the Alamo. The historic mission had been reconstructed to its original size and features. Bullet holes from the battle were still visible inside the Alamo itself. Memorabilia from Colonel William Travis were encased along with his last letter seeking reinforcements.

She read the words of his letter, signed, *Victory or Death.* The chapel seemed hallowed and a bit eerie to Angela. She felt a pervasive sadness on the grounds, and the silence seemed a mute testimony to the heroism and tragedy of that March day one hundred and sixty some years ago. In the courtyard stood a giant, lonely live oak tree.

"Do you suppose it was here during the battle?" she asked.

"It looks like it could have been, although there's no marker to indicate it."

Other tourists milled in the courtyard and maintained the quiet, respectful demeanor befitting the grounds. The atmosphere, to Angela, seemed as heavy and emotional as a cemetery, although no headstones were evident.

Outside of the Alamo's stone walls, the streets were charged with life. Cars, trolleys, pedestrians and activity removed the weighted feelings Angela left behind at the Alamo. They stopped at a restaurant and sipped iced tea beneath the shade of the canvas awning. Angela stirred her drink with a long spoon. "Do you suppose he realized how outnumbered they were?"

"Travis?" Chip drew on his straw. "I'm sure he did, at the last. There's still controversy over his holding the Alamo. Some say his pride and ambitions wouldn't let him admit defeat, though he knew it was suicide."

"Was it his sense of duty and obligation, or his vanity?"

"There've been studies in the past that argue that very point. He was a determined young man, proud, maybe vain, definitely driven. He died a hero, though. Took a lot of good men with him."

Angela's brows furrowed as she pondered the Alamo's commander in charge. "He was young, a newcomer, probably had to prove himself, I suppose. I can certainly relate to all that."

Chip took her hand. "Texas was a land hard fought and hard won, Angel. It's part of our past that a lot of people don't understand. The pioneers who homesteaded and tamed this land, had to fight for it all the way."

"Like your great-grandfather?"

"All my father's people and those before him. They're tough, they're hearty and they're true."

"It's kind of nice, Chip, knowing that you come from that kind of background. I can't wait to meet your parents."

Chip smiled. "They're gonna love you." *Just like I do.* He studied the woman beside him, not wanting to distract her interest in all of the sights, sounds and smells of the evening. The faint scent of cherry blossoms, magnolia, and spruce wafted on the breeze. The air began to soften with the lengthening shadows of evening. Cicadas and birds in the trees blended their individual chatter into pleasant songs. *How can a man be so lucky? How can I make this last?*

"Let's take a ride on the canal, shall we?" Chip suggested. "We can float past all the riverside restaurants, and you can decide where you'd like to eat."

"I'm with you."

They clambered down cement steps and the costumed boatmen welcomed them aboard. Once settled among the other passengers, they began a leisurely ride through the canal that wound around the streets of old San Antonio.

Weeping willow trees draped sleepy strands of leaves toward the water. The banks were landscaped with indigenous plants that would be equally at home in Texas or old

Mexico. From a bridge arched high above the canal, a mariachi band played soft, romantic tunes for the passengers. The trees were decorated with miniature crystal lights that blinked on and off, as the branches swayed in rhythm to a gentle Texas breeze. In all, it was a peaceful, lovely evening.

They passed several restaurants with open-air porticos near the River Walk. When the boat ride ended, Chip and Angela sought out a restaurant that boasted prime rib and authentic old Mexican cuisine. Angela enjoyed the serenity and simplicity of the city and all its amenities. It was an evening designed for romance. And if her heart was to be believed, she truly was falling in love.

"Tell me, Chip. Is there anything about you a woman wouldn't love?"

"I've been told I shouldn't leave my shaving gear out when I'm through."

"Separate bathrooms."

"I tend to be a little lazy on Sunday mornings," he added.

"That's a crime?"

"I'm not too keen about mowing lawns."

"That's what teenagers are for," Angela suggested.

"I like to fish when I'm not chasing angels."

"That could be a problem."

"Being a pilot means I'm gone quite a bit."

"Breathing room," she declared. "It's good for any relationship."

"I'm not perfect, Angel, but I aim to please."

"I'd like to reciprocate, Captain."

"Darlin', you already have."

The waiter appeared as if on cue, removed their plates and offered dessert. Both declined.

"What do you say we turn in? We'll have a long day tomorrow, I guarantee."

Angela leaned on his arm, content to feel his warmth against her skin. If nights like this were in the future with Captain Stephens, the prospect wasn't all bad.

Chip hailed a cab to the hotel. They rode the glass elevator to the top of the hotel, and strolled out to the overlook and took in the entire view of the city. It was a vast, magical panorama that Angela compared to movie scenes and special effects. "It's so beautiful, Chip. What a wonderful city."

"I'm glad you like it. I'd do anything to make memories like this with you." Chip circled his arms around her and pulled her back against him.

Angela nestled her head into the hollow of his shoulder. "It feels so good to be with you, Chip. I felt this way in Kauai too."

Someday. Chip thought. *Someday soon.* "Do you think the stars are as bright in Texas as they are in Colorado?"

Angela looked up at the few stars that were evident in the spacious Texas sky. "Could be the lights of the city are dimming them. It's always brighter out in the open."

"I would have bet that Texas stars were brighter, being bigger than everyone else's."

"What are the odds?" she asked.

"Let's say—ten to one."

Angela turned in his arms to face him. She playfully kissed him and said, "That, Captain Stephens, is a bet."

Unlike the bright blue Colorado skies she was used to, Angela rose to a balmy, overcast sky. She drew the curtains fully open and allowed the muted light inside her suite. Looking out over the sprawling city, still quiet in the early morning hour, she imagined how it might have looked on the eve of the Alamo battle one hundred and sixty years ago. A fine mist hung over the low buildings as if a celestial blanket was draped over the peaceful, sleeping giant. As far as she could see there were no mountains, unlike the formidable, massive Rockies that greeted her from her bay window each morning. It was easy to enjoy this time off, but the Center nagged at her conscience. Was Richie handling their station with a new person? Was he staying out of Rankin's way? She pushed the edgy thoughts aside as the phone rang.

"Mornin', Angel."

"Good morning to you."

"You ready for breakfast?"

"Give me a half-hour." She was more than ready to meet Captain Stephens and get on with the day.

Chapter Seven

Chip swung the car onto the busy highway heading north. Highrises, townhouse villages, and industrial complexes soon gave way to the green rolling hills outside of the city.

"How far away are we?" she asked.

"About two hours. Some of the prettiest country in Texas." Chip patted her hand. "I had about the best childhood a kid could want. I learned to fish, swim, hunt and ride horses before I was six years old. How about you? You said you used to ride. How long ago?"

"I quit riding when I was about fifteen, but I used to fancy myself a pretty fair barrel-racer."

Chip smiled. "I think Pops was riding before he could walk. He'd rather take his big bay to town than his pickup truck."

"And your mother?"

"She has a sedan." A few minutes passed without either

speaking before Chip broke the silence. "So, your parents are divorced?"

"Yes, but it took a long time. Dad once said he couldn't live with her and couldn't live without her. I think they loved each other, though." Angela sighed. "They never really discussed it with me, but looking back I think my mother tried to be a good farm wife. It just didn't work. She should never have left the city. After I graduated high school she remarried."

"Hmmm." Chip frowned. "That's a sad way to bring up a child."

"I can identify with how your Bobby Ray must have felt—losing his mother, I mean—" Angela paused. "I lost my mother, too. When she decided to leave my dad, she distanced herself not only from him but from me."

"So you stayed with your father then?"

"Dad and I seemed to understand each other. He's a no-nonsense kind of guy. Big, strong—but not very easy to talk to. Doesn't let anyone get too close to him."

"Not even you?"

"I left home when I was eighteen. I only go back to visit once in a while."

"No sisters? No brothers?"

"No."

"Me, either. Mama used to say God only handed out one angel at a time."

"Your mother called you an angel?"

Chip laughed. "She got to where she didn't believe it after a while. But," he squeezed her hand, "I suspect she'll recognize *my* angel when she meets you."

They drove through white, rocky hills dotted by thick scrub oak. The ravines were coarse with rock, layered by multi-colored ribbons of minerals. The scrub oak gave way to cottonwoods and live oak trees that bordered the Medina River.

"Our place isn't far now," he explained. "The fenceline begins just a little over that ridge. You'll see it on the left when we reach the crest."

Angela felt an unusual fluttering in her stomach. She realized she was becoming nervous. "I feel like I'm about to take a test."

"Don't be scared. If you don't feel at home the minute you get there, I'll be very surprised."

Chip pointed out a rudimentary fencing on the left. "This is some of the original fence my great-grandfather's hands put up."

"It sure lasted a long time. Is that oak or spruce?"

"Cedar. Over a hundred years old."

Angela saw an old abandoned house surrounded by a cluster of trees. "What's that?"

"Great-grandpa's old homestead. He built that for his bride before they married."

"It's still standing?"

"We use it if we get caught in a storm. It was a cozy little home at one time. They raised all four of their boys in that little two-room house."

"Oh my, that *would* be cozy."

Chip laughed. "From what I understand, great-grandma couldn't keep the boys inside very long. They preferred to sleep out under the trees when they got big enough to be out on their own. Three of the four left the ranch. But my grandpa Mitchell stayed on."

"You've got a long history here, Chip. That must be nice—having roots."

"We do have our roots here on the *Double S*. My great grandfather, Rose—"

"Rose?"

"Rosamond. Everyone called him Rose. He took the *Double S* brand for their name, Stephens, but also out of respect for the Comanche." Chip drew a double S sign in the air. "The sign of the snake. The Comanche didn't molest Rose when they saw his brand, which was what they considered their sign. Great-grandpa let them take a steer or two and they left him alone. It was an agreeable relationship."

"Comanches! I guess they were still pretty active when he was here, huh?"

"A little too active. There was plenty of discontent when Grandpa Rose settled here. All a part of our history."

Chip turned onto a well-worn dirt road that was just wide enough for the big Lincoln to navigate. "The main house is just up here aways."

Angela watched, fascinated, as a herd of goats trotted away from the noise and dust of the car. "Those look like Angora goats! Are they?"

"Yep. Mama keeps them for the hair. This is sheep and goat country, as well as Herefords." He honked his horn twice and pulled into the circular drive in front of a modest ranch-style brick home. "There's Mama now."

A thin woman of medium height emerged from the front door, wiping her hands on her apron. Mrs. Stephens looked about sixty. Short blonde hair mixed with silver curled softly around her smiling face.

Chip turned off the ignition, leaned over and kissed Angela on the cheek. "They're gonna love you."

Chip's assurances didn't arrest Angela's unaccustomed shyness, but she waited as he opened her door and steeled herself to meet his folks.

With his hand at the small of her back, Chip escorted

Angela to the front porch where his mother stood. Mrs. Stephens didn't wait for an introduction, but grasped Angela by the shoulders and hugged her. "Welcome to our home, Angela. I've heard so much about you!"

Angela smelled the subtle perfume Mrs. Stephens wore, mixed with the scent of cinnamon and apples.

"Welcome home, dear." Mrs. Stephens hugged her son, then took both of their hands. "Well, don't stand out here, let's go inside and get acquainted."

Chip grinned at Angela as his mother walked inside. "I told you," he whispered. "Fearsome as a lamb."

Angela felt relieved by the warm welcome. *Perhaps meeting Chip's folks won't be as bad as facing a firing squad, after all.* They followed Mrs. Stephens inside. The main room was a combination living and dining room. Spacious yet unpretentious, the room held an assortment of heavy maple furniture, a stark contrast to Angela's austere contemporary furnishings. Mrs. Stephens seemed to prefer the simplicity of early American antiques.

"I've got tea ready," Mrs. Stephens announced. "Angela, would you care for tea or coffee?"

Angela and Chip seated themselves around the kitchen table. It was apparent that this was the preferred room for entertaining guests. "I'll have tea, thank you."

"Coffee for me," Chip ordered.

"Just like your father." Mrs. Stephens clucked. "I swear that man could go through a gallon of coffee a day."

"I like it," a man's voice boomed.

Angela jumped at the unexpected sound and looked behind her to see a giant of a man striding into the room. The cowboy boots and large straw hat added at least another six inches to his height and exaggerated his size. The big man extended a bear-size paw and gingerly pumped her hand.

"So you're the girl I've been hearing so much about."

Angela felt a blush rise in her neck and fan to her cheeks.

"Now, Mitch, don't scare her to death," Mrs. Stephens chided as she placed a teapot in front of Angela. "And take that hat off in here. You know better."

The big man complied as easily as a well-mannered child. "I've been waitin' a long time to meet you, little lady. I understand you saved our boy's life."

"Pops doesn't mince words, Angel." Chip's eyes glittered the same cornflower blue as his mother's, with a hint of mischief that was definitely his father's. "Do you, Pops?"

"Never was much for circling a target when you can shoot straight at it. Takes too much effort." His voice was deep and commanding, yet kind. Angela immediately liked the old man.

"So where's Bobby Ray? Did he know I was coming in this weekend?"

Mrs. Stephens shifted in her chair. "He said they'd be back late Sunday afternoon."

"Good. I wanted him to meet Angela."

"He would have been here, but this was their big spring trip to Houston."

"How big is his graduating class?" Angela asked.

"Twenty five, I believe. Twenty six if that Rodgers boy catches up."

"You've got a name besides Angel?" Pops interrupted.

"Angela Lawrey."

"Mitchell Rosamond Stephens. But you can call me Pops."

Angela smiled.

"I'm Dorothy." Mrs. Stephens placed a delicate china saucer and teacup in front of her guest. "Thank you for coming to visit."

"It's my pleasure." Angela glanced at Chip. It was clear he was enjoying the scene he had created. He looked amused and relaxed.

After she had served coffee, Dorothy opened the conversation. "Robert tells us you're an air traffic controller. That sounds very . . . challenging."

Pops leaned back in his chair and sipped his mug of coffee. "This is the nineties Dorie. Women do all kinds of hard work. Isn't that right?" Pops asked Angela.

The young woman nodded and sipped her tea. *Cinnamon and apple. One of my favorites.*

"I was raised on a farm outside Weeping Water, Nebraska," Angela explained. "I graduated from the university in Oklahoma City, and I've been in Colorado ever since. I've done my share of farm work. *That* was hard work."

"Well then, Angel. You know how to ride?"

"Yes."

"I guess you wouldn't mind riding a horse with me then?" Pops looked very pleased with himself.

"I'd like that."

"All right!" He banged his open hand on the table in front of him and Angela, startled, jumped in response. Pops shoved his large frame away from the table and stood, towering over their guest. "Well, c'mon. The day's half gone."

"She just got here, Mitchell. Let her finish her tea, for goodness sake!"

"You don't want her to puff up like a blowfish. You've had enough there, haven't you?"

"Yes, sir."

"What about me?" Chip asked. "Am I invited?"

"I don't recollect you being asked, son. You keep your mama company. I'll bring Angel back alive. Come out to the barn when you're ready. I'll saddle up the mare for you."

"The paint?" Chip confirmed. "Don't you think—"

"She says she knows how to ride."

"Now, Mitchell—"

"Honey, hold supper for us. We'll be back before too long."

"Which direction are you headed?" Mrs. Stephens asked.

"North line." With that Pops slipped his hat on and disappeared out the back door.

"My goodness. Please don't mind him, Angela. He's not used to having guests." Mrs. Stephens looked slightly unsettled as she tried to explain her husband's rash behavior.

"That's okay." The young woman chuckled. "I would enjoy a little fresh air, and the ride will do me good."

"Are you sure?" Chip asked.

"I'll be okay," Angela assured him. She quickly gulped the tea that remained in her cup and dabbed her lips with the cloth napkin Mrs. Stephens had provided. "That was very nice, Mrs. Stephens—I mean, Dorothy. Excuse me, I'd better change."

"We'll have a chance to visit this evening, I hope," Dorothy said. "You two go along. Mitchell will be waiting."

Angela and Chip retrieved their bags from the car, and Chip led her to a guest bedroom. "Looks like my mother made everything up for you."

An ornately carved rosewood headboard matched the bow-front dresser and mirror next to the bed. An assortment of miniature pink roses and delicate white flowers, that must have come from Dorothy's garden, graced the highly polished dresser top. Next to the window, a rosewood nightstand guarded the corner, adorned with an old-fashioned brass and glass lamp.

"Chip, it's beautiful!"

"My mother likes antiques, as you can see. I guess that's how I acquired my appreciation of old-fashioned things."

"Your mother has exquisite taste."

"I'll let her know you said so." He drew her close and hugged her gently.

"What are you going to do while I'm gone?" she asked.

"We'll catch up on Bobby Ray's doings and get dinner ready. I'm sure she has something special in mind."

"You help out in the kitchen?"

"I love to cook—on occasion," he qualified. "When I've got time to sit down long enough to enjoy it."

"Another point in your favor, Captain."

Several horses milled in the corral as Chip led her to the barn. Pops was saddling up the paint as they entered the large, airy stable.

"There's an extra hat in the tack room," Pops instructed. "You didn't bring one, did you?"

"No, sir. I didn't."

"Dorie's ought to fit you."

He turned and faced the young woman. "Here. Slide on up here and see if I got those stirrups right."

Without hesitating, Angela grasped the saddle horn, plowed her booted foot into the stirrup and swung her leg high over the back of the paint mare. She settled into the saddle and fit both feet into the stirrups.

"A little short," Pops snorted. "I'll adjust them for you. Just sit tight."

Chip handed a softly curled straw cowboy hat up to her. "See if that fits."

Angela placed it on her head and snugged it down. "Just right. Thanks. Is this your mother's?"

"Bobby Ray's. Mom's looked a little small."

"That's a workin' saddle. Is that comfortable for you?" Pops asked.

Angela nodded.

Chip led her out of the barn into the bright Texas sunshine. Pops followed, leading a big thoroughbred stallion.

"How's Brownie doing, anyway?" Chip asked.

"He's just fine. We've been chasing calves, haven't we, boy?" The man proudly patted his neck, and the horse responded by lifting his muzzle upward. His well-groomed mane and tail were a shiny coal-black, and his skin quivered at the man's gentle touch. "That paint's lively, so don't give her too much lead," Pops warned Angela. "She can be skittish, but just let her know who's boss."

"I'll do my best."

Chip appeared slightly concerned. "Let Pops know when you've had enough, okay?"

Angela nodded. "We'll be all right."

"You're not going to take her by the river, Pops?"

"Nah. We've got a full moon tonight, and I've got to check the fence on the north end."

"Okay." Chip slapped the back of his father's big bay. "Take care of her."

"Don't you worry 'bout that. We'll be back for supper." Pops wheeled his dark brown horse around and backed it in reverse as easily as a youngster might handle a hot rod. "Come on, Angel. Let's ride."

Angela clucked twice and heeled the paint, following Pop's direction. As they headed into the pasture the little paint seemed eager to run. Angela allowed her to catch up to Pops so they could ride side by side.

"What's her name, Pops?"

"We call her Paint, but she comes to anything. You can whistle if she's out in the field and she'll know you're talking to her."

Angela stroked the horse's mane, a mix of white and brown. "She's a pretty horse."

"She's lively. I guess that's why Robert was concerned. But you look like you can handle her."

Angela appreciated the old man's observation. It was a good start.

"Weeping Water?" Pops drawled. "Where in the heck is that?"

"Between Lincoln and Omaha."

"Get home often?"

Angela sighed. It had been years since she had felt comfortable on the farm; years since she had visited. "Not really. Dad came to Oklahoma when I graduated and I haven't been home for quite a while."

"Hummph," Pops grunted. "Trouble at home?"

"No. I just haven't been back."

That answer obviously didn't sit well with Mitchell Rosamond. "My boy gets home once or twice a month. I'd be confounded if I had a daughter and she didn't get to see me. Bobby Ray's planning to stay on the ranch after high school—unless he goes to college, of course, but he'll be with us 'til then."

"How is Bobby Ray doing in school?" Angela asked, relieved to change the subject.

"He's doing fine. He and Dorie work on homework almost every night. He'll be graduating mid-June. Are you coming back for his graduation?"

"I don't know. Chip and I didn't discuss it."

"Well, it'd be a shame for you to miss it. Dorie's planning a big to-do. That boy's about as close to being our own son as Rob was. We raised him from a baby, ya see."

Loping alongside Pops, Angela nodded in rhythm to her mare's gait. "Chip told me about his wife and the accident."

"It was tragic. I never saw a couple of kids so in love. It took my son years to get over the loss. But little Bobby Ray didn't know any different. Dorie took real good care of him."

"It must've been hard—on all of you."

"Nah. One thing you learn out here, Angel. God knows what he's doin', and there's a reason for everything. Every day's a blessing as far as I can tell. Me and Dorie always wanted another child, and I guess this was His way of providin' it. Not the way we wanted it, mind you, but I ain't one to question the ways of the Lord."

Pops' words tugged at a spot deep in her heart. Comparing her lack of connection and warmth with her parents to the closeness of Chip's family left her feeling detached and cold underneath the bright Texas sky.

They rode into a field dotted with cactus which were budding with small blossoms of yellow, pink and red. Juniper vied for the rocky soil alongside gnarled oak trees twisting scrawny arms toward the sky.

"A little bit of heaven," Pops announced. "If I didn't cultivate the southern pasture, it would look just like this— wild juniper, prickly pear cactus, oak and weeds."

A long-tailed black bird swooped between the two riders, and landed in a nearby oak. Its high-pitched squawking sounded as if it was scolding them for intruding in its territory.

"I saw some goats when we came in. Does Dorothy gather the wool herself?"

"A local family shears the goats. Dorie likes to help out, but they do the bulk of the work. Dorie used to dye wool from plants she gathered on the ranch, but now a family takes care of all of that. They do some fine weaving."

After a few minutes Pops asked, "Did Rob tell you about Grandpa Rose's sons?"

"A little. He mentioned there were four boys."

"David, Robert, Mitchell, and Lewis. The oldest two ran off as soon as they were old enough. Mitchell stayed on the ranch, and Lewis was the only one who went to school and amounted to anything."

"The banker?"

"Yep. Went to college in Austin, then came back and started the Lone Star Bank. I'm named after my father, Mitchell, and my grandfather, Rosamond. He had brothers who settled in Virginia and Louisiana, but that's all we know about them. Grampa Rose was more adventurous and wound up in Texas. In fact, he was a bit of a maverick."

"He'd have to be, coming here in the eighteen sixties."

"Peaceful here, ain't it?"

"It's very nice. Beautiful country."

"Can't imagine how anybody can give up something like this and move away to the city."

"You mean Ch—Robert?"

"Well, he never completely gave up the ranch. I just mean folks in general. I never could live in the city. This here's as close to heaven a body can get."

"I believe it."

"Bobby Ray says he wants to be a rancher. That'd make me real proud. But Dorie and Rob think he should go to college first."

"He could get a good background in animal husbandry or agriculture."

"Don't make much sense to me. But I guess there's a whole lot more to know about ranchin' nowadays." Pops' face grew thoughtful. "Lord knows I just raised cattle and crops by the seat of my pants and God's good nature. Fortunately, He saw fit to keep me and my family well fed."

Angela smiled. She envied the roots he had in this land, that ran as deep as those of the ancient oak. She could almost imagine his sense of kinship with the earth over which they rode.

"It's wide open up here, Angel. Let's go." Pops clucked his tongue and the large bay broke into a gallop.

Paint needed no encouragement. The horse pulled against the reins to keep up with Brownie. Angela let her take over and enjoyed the rhythm of the little mare as they galloped over the field. The breeze teased tendrils from beneath her hat, and she felt as free and unfettered as the birds that soared overhead.

As far as she could see, miles of rocky, untamed land spread before them, as open and natural as Grandpa Rose must have found it. She imagined the young cowboy roaming this land for game and edible plants. It must have been a beautiful time to be alive.

Pops' long legged stallion out-distanced them, and the little paint struggled against Angela for release. "Come on, Paint. Go get 'em." The paint bolted forward, racing to catch the thoroughbred. She caught sight of Pops, suddenly reining left. Angela stiffened and pulled in the reins as she caught sight of an unusual movement. It looked like two long-stemmed plants blowing in the breeze, but upon closer inspection it became clear the swaying pair were not plants at all.

"Rein 'er in, Angel," Pops bellowed. "Those are rattlers!"

Chapter Eight

"Whoa, Paint!" Pulling back on the reins, Angela tried to regain control but the mare resisted and turned her head in annoyance, continuing to charge. Angela gasped. Her breath seemed to halt in her chest. She jerked the reins harder, shortening Paint's lead about the same time the mare must have seen the danger.

The snakes stood close to four feet high, their tails coiled around each other. Large rattles were in evidence and their thick, diamond-patterned bodies undulated in a menacing, macabre dance. Their heads struck close to each other then drew back, weaving and bobbing, seemingly oblivious to the horse and rider.

The mare screamed and reared up, then slammed back to the earth and bucked, trying to dislodge saddle and rider. Angela held her seat and stayed with the panicked paint as it charged left. They bolted past junipers and sagebrush, and the horse raced toward a low-branched oak. Angela hunched against the mare's neck and barely escaped the

tree. The paint was fully undone and chose to flee as far
and as fast as her legs would allow. The landscape blurred
in Angela's sight, but she held on.

She understood the mare's need to flee and allowed her
to race out of harm's way before she tried, again, to subdue
her. Angela heard the thundering hooves of Pops' big thoroughbred, and heard him curse the mare, the rattlers, and
himself as they closed in.

"Whoa, Paint. Whoa." Angela reined tight and finally got
control of the mare and eased her to a stop. Pops pulled up
beside her, red-faced and worried.

"Are you all right?" He swore at the paint.

"We're fine." Angela patted the lathered neck of the
mare and spoke to her, soothing and slow. "We're okay,
aren't we, girl?"

"I'm sorry, Angel."

"It's okay. We had a fun little ride. Didn't we, girl?"
Angela continued patting the mare and stroking her.

"You saw those rattlers?"

"Yes, but I don't think Paint did 'til the last minute.
What were they doing?"

"Combat dance. People used to think it was a mating
ritual, but they were actually sizing each other up."

Pops dismounted and checked the mare for any sign of
injury. "I don't think they got her."

Angela looked behind her, but the snakes were no longer
in view. "I didn't think I'd see any snakes out here, but I
guess they're all over, aren't they?"

"I see 'em on occasion."

Pops also seemed to have calmed down now that they
were clearly out of danger. He narrowed a wise and weath-
ered gaze on Angela and a smile returned to his face.
"You're a heck of a horsewoman, Angel."

Angela gulped back the tears that welled in her eyes. Not even her father had praised her horsemanship to that degree. She swiped at a tear that escaped her. "Thanks, Pops."

"I guess we should head back."

"What?"

"We've had enough excitement, I reckon."

"We've got a fence line to check, don't we?" Angela peered over at her mount, satisfied that the mare was calmed. She stroked it's long neck. "You don't need to quit on my account. We're ready, aren't we, girl?"

Pops pulled at the front of his hat, his smile as wide as the brim of the straw Stetson he wore. " 'Atta girl. Let's go."

When they got back to the stable, Chip was on hand to help her dismount and corral the horses. He handed her a brush and they both worked on the mare, while Pops attended to his horse.

"Mighty fine rider, you've got there," Pops complimented his son. "As good as any I've seen."

"Oh yeah?" Chip peered over the top of the paint at Angela. "Pretty high praise coming from a Texan. What did you do to deserve that?"

"Nothing." Angela grinned.

"I'm gonna wash up, son. I suppose you and your mama have supper on?"

"Yes, sir."

"You come along when you're ready, then. I'll let Dorie know we're back."

Pops ambled off, cowboy hat intact, looking like a man who was fully a part of the land.

"Your dad's a wonderful man. Gentle, funny, wise." She sighed. "It's nice being here, Chip."

"I told you, didn't I?" Chip moved around the front of the paint and removed the brush from her hand. Pulling her into his arms, he hugged her.

"What?"

"You'd fall in love with them and then you'd have to marry me."

"Is that a proposal, Captain Stephens?" Angela raised her smiling face to his and allowed Chip to remove the straw Stetson from her head. Her thick, dark ponytail fell to her shoulders. Chip tugged at the elastic band and slid it from her hair. She shook her hair free and pressed her face against his chest. She could feel the steady beat of his heart and the warmth of his skin beneath the cotton shirt he wore.

"I don't think I've quite convinced you yet." Chip kissed her lightly.

"I'll give you about a year to stop that," she teased.

"How about fifty?"

A scraggly-looking Australian shepherd nosed up to Chip, barking and jumping.

"Hey, boy, where've you been? Out chasin' rabbits?" Chip released Angela and bent to pet the dog. The plumed black and white tail beat furiously against Angela's leg.

"A little jealous?" The dog looked up at Angela then focused again on Chip. "Bobby Ray's dog. Didn't want us too close, apparently. Say hi to Jasper."

Angela held her hand out, allowing the animal to sniff. "Hey, boy. Were you looking out for me?" The dog panted, and wagged his tail. "Good dog." Turning to Chip, she asked, "How can you stand to leave here?"

"I don't leave for long."

"I bet it breaks your mother's heart when you have to go."

"She's got Bobby Ray and Pops to baby-sit. And all her animals."

"But she misses you."

"I love the ranch, Angel, but it's not my home anymore."

"You'd give this up?"

"I already have. Pops will pass it along to Bobby Ray when he's ready."

"You're not going to live in Los Angeles all your life, are you? I mean California is nice and all but—"

"I think Mama's got supper ready." Chip smiled mysteriously and squeezed her. "Come on. You'll have time to wash up and change, if you like." He grasped her hand and they walked together into the house.

Once inside, the smell of fresh-baked bread greeted them. The dining room table was beautifully set. Excusing herself, Angela hurried to shower and change before supper was served. She had brought along a peach colored blouse and skirt, detailed with hand-crocheted edging on the blouse. She brushed her dark hair until it gleamed and wore it loose around her shoulders.

When she emerged, she met Chip and Pops in the family room. Dorothy joined them with iced tea.

"You had a little scare, Angela. Are you all right?" Dorothy asked.

"What do you mean?" Chip interrupted. "What happened?"

"Nothing this little girl couldn't handle. You should have seen her, son. You were right about that paint, though. I should have known better."

Chip reached for Angela's hand, concern etching his face. "Did she throw you?"

"She tried," Angela admitted. "She gave me quite a ride."

"Like a bat outta badlands," Pops roared. "I never saw that paint move so fast, that freckle-faced, pint-sized—"

"Now, Mitchell," Dorothy soothed.

"We came across a pair of bull rattlers on the north ridge. Almost scared the bejeezus outta me and Brownie, then up comes that paint, chargin' to beat the band."

"You ran into snakes?" Chip paled. "Why didn't you say something? I didn't know."

Angela shrugged.

"She rode that mare like she'd been born in a saddle, son. You didn't tell me this little girl was a regular Annie Oakley. I tell ya, I've never seen anything like it."

"Thank goodness you weren't injured, honey. I never would have forgiven myself."

"If that little girl can boss big planes out of the sky, she can sure handle a little scrape with a rattler."

"That took a lot of courage, dear," Dorothy added. "A *lot* of courage."

Angela squirmed. "Paint's a lively little horse. She did all the work—I just hung on."

"We ought to get rid of that horse before someone gets hurt." Chip's face hardened.

"No! Pops warned me not to give her too much rein. It was my fault. She likes to run. I let her go a little, and before I knew it we ran into those snakes. She did what comes naturally to an animal, that's all." When she had finished, Angela realized her voice had been quaking and her muscles were as tight as the reins she'd pulled against Paint. Her hands began shaking. Trying to be inconspicuous, she folded them in her lap. "I'm sorry. I know she's not my horse. It just wasn't her fault."

"Angel, honey, you did just fine. Rob's a little overprotective, you see, and I understand that. But that little mare's stayin' right here so you can ride her the next time you're out. You got my word on it."

Angela exhaled, relieved. Her rigid body sagged into the chair. It was as if she had been transported back in time onto her father's farm in Nebraska—only then she had lost the argument.

"Well, y'all, let's eat before supper gets cold," Dorothy suggested. "Robert, if you'll show our guest to the table, I'll set the food out."

"Now, Angel—" Pops tried to continue.

"Mitchell."

"Ah, excuse me. I better help Dorie in the kitchen." Pops hauled himself out of the leather recliner and followed his wife, leaving his chair rocking in his wake.

Angela stole a glance at Chip and sighed self-consciously. "I'm sorry, Chip. I didn't want to worry you."

He circled his arm around her and lifted her hand to his lips. "Honey, I don't want any harm to come to you." A shade of pain tinted the pilot's blue eyes, and Angela realized he was also reacting to a past trauma. Only that one had taken his wife.

"I broke my leg when the horse I was training fell with me," Angela explained. "Mom had already left us and my father . . ." Angela bit her lip. "I guess he didn't want to lose me too. He sold my horse and I never rode again. I thought he was punishing me at the time, but I guess he was trying to protect me."

Chip nodded. "We try to wrap those we love in a safety net, but it doesn't always work that way does it, darlin'?"

She shook her head. "Fate, luck, accidents. Who knows why things happen the way they do."

"Well, if it was fate that brought us together, I'll be eternally grateful."

"Supper's on," Pops boomed.

Chip rose and pulled Angela with him. "Let's see what you think about my cookin'."

When they had seated themselves, Dorothy nodded at her husband and said, "Mitchell, if you'll say grace—"

Pops cleared his throat. "Yes'm."

The four grasped hands and bowed their heads. "Dear Lord, thank you for this good food and family. We especially thank you for the angel who sits among us . . ." Dorothy smiled, approving her husband's blessing, then he continued.

"Bless the meat and blast the skin, back your ears and dive in!"

Dorothy gasped. "Mitchell, please. We have a guest here!"

"She's family, Dorie. And it's about time, ain't it, son?"

"Yes, sir," Chip agreed, smiling. "It's past time."

Angela choked as she tried to suppress a laugh and Chip squeezed her hand.

"Would you pass the chicken, Dorie?" Pops asked. "Angel, here, is hungry."

After dinner, Pops and Dorothy seated themselves on the porch swing and sat, hand-in-hand, like a couple of teens. It was a cool, crisp Texas night. Miles below the ranch house, Angela could see the rolling, rocky hills that led to the Guadalupe.

"The moon's out," Pops announced. "Take her on down to the river, son. It'll be a nice ride."

Chip searched Angela's face. "Want to?"

"I'd love it."

"This time—"

"I'd like to ride Paint," she added.

"Honey, we've got tamer horses. I wouldn't want to risk—"

"Paint is fine, Chip. I like that little horse."

Chip shook his head. "I can see right now you've got a stubborn streak I'm not going to tangle with."

"I'll change and meet you down there."

Angela darted into the house and quickly changed into a pair of jeans, a T-shirt, and jacket. She jogged down the path that led to the stable and found Chip saddling a gelding. She spied the saddle she had used earlier, hanging on a wooden workhorse in the tack room.

"I'll lift it on for you," Chip told her. "Go ahead and get her ready."

Patiently, the little horse stood and allowed Angela to fit the bridle into her mouth and draw it over her ears. Angela stroked the mare's muzzle as she led her from her stall. After they had saddled their mounts, Chip led the horses into the yard.

"Have a good ride, y'all," Dorothy called.

"We'll look for you by midnight, Rob," Pops added.

Angela and Chip followed a well-worn path leading south toward the river. Bobby Ray's dog, Jasper, sped ahead of the horses, barking and circling back, then racing away again. Moonlight filtered through the cottonwoods that lined the Guadalupe, shining on rocks and lazy water.

When they reached the river's edge, Chip stopped by a grassy area that opened up into a meadow.

"Come on down, darlin'."

Angela swung her leg over the back of Paint. Chip placed his hands around her waist and steadied her as she descended and found her footing. She turned in his grasp, clasping her hands behind his neck, facing him.

"Angela, honey—"

"Sh-sh-sh." She placed a finger on his lips. "Don't say anything." Leaning forward, she kissed him. Slowly, softly, silently. The world vanished as Angela fell into the spell her Texas cowboy had cast.

Ever so gently, she drew back and moved her hands to his chest. She could feel his heart beneath her hands that lay on his western shirt.

"I didn't think it possible but—" she whispered. "Chip, I think I love you."

"Honey, I *know* I love you. There's no guessing, on my part."

"What am I going to do with you?" She sighed.

"Well, we've got the hard part figured out. We just have to decide what to do next."

"You live in Los Angeles," she reminded him. "That's easy?"

"We're going to get married as soon as we can," he began. "And honey, I know it's old-fashioned of me, but I'm not going to marry you until I've built our house."

"But I have a house—a condo—in Longmont. We could live there if you can commute by plane to L.A."

Chip shook his head. "*Our* house. I don't mean to be hard-headed about this, Angel. But it's the way my father and his father and his father before him did it. Maybe I'm just superstitious, but I want our house finished before I ask you to move in with me."

"But Chip, this is the nineties, remember?"

Chip took her hands in his. "Darlin', I love you. And I told you before, I'm old-fashioned enough that I want to make this right. Will you marry me?"

Angela blinked back tears that threatened. "How can you be so sure it's right for us?"

"We may have some adjustments," Chip reckoned. "Every saddle needs a bit of cinching here and there . . ."

"Are you comparing me to a pack horse, Chip Stevens?"

"No way, honey." He kissed her brow. "It's just that I've been there before, and I know that no matter how much you love someone there's always going to be some itch that'll need scratching."

"You have such a way about you," she teased. "How can I resist?"

"You mean you will?"

Chip's face looked as hopeful and vulnerable as a teen on a first date. "Of course I will," she smiled. "I was wondering how long this courtship thing would last."

Chip enveloped her in his strong arms and kissed her like a man who had finally reached the end of a long journey. "Not too much longer, I hope." Chip kissed her slowly this time. "We'll work out the details later."

Angela became aware of the cicadas buzzing in the trees and the horses munching noisily on tall grass. A slight breeze fanned the branches and leaves of the big trees that encircled them. It was difficult for her, a strong-willed, determined, independent young woman to take the backseat to decisions that involved her so directly.

"Are you sure?" she asked. "You want to wait?"

"You won't regret it, honey. I'll make you the happiest woman alive."

Angela felt her stomach tighten. *Would we have the kind of marriage that Dorothy and Pops seemed to share, or would ours end in a deadlock as my parents' had*? It scared her to think of the gravity of her commitment.

"Where will we live?" she ventured.

"I'm working that out."

"California?"

"I wouldn't think of asking you to leave Colorado," he soothed.

"Longmont, then?"

"Don't worry your pretty head about it tonight." He kissed her forehead, cheeks and chin. "It's enough that we've agreed to marry."

Chip took the reins that trailed the grass in front of Paint. "We better head back."

Woodenly, Angela allowed Chip to steady her horse as she mounted it. *Was I dreaming? Did Chip actually ask me to marry him? A man I've met only a month ago. Have I gone completely mad?*

Chip wore a smile as bright as the full moon above them. "Come on, darlin'. Let's go tell the folks."

Pops and Dorothy still sat on the porch when Angela and Chip rode up on their horses. She now understood that the hitching posts in front of the house were functional and not just a part of the ranch-style décor.

"Didn't get lost, huh?" Pops joked.

"No, sir. I think I got found instead."

"What do you mean, dear?" Mrs. Stephens asked.

Chip circled his arm around Angela and together they walked up the steps to the porch. "Mama? Pops?" he started. "Angela and I are going to be married."

Chip's parents were on their feet and circled the pair before Angela had time to react. Pops gave her the biggest bear hug she'd ever had, while Dorothy hugged Chip and then reached for Angela.

"You don't know how happy we are," she said. "You seem so perfect for our Robert."

"I hope so," Angela stammered.

"Well, son, I hoped your Angel was real. By golly she is. Rock solid."

Angela warmed to Pops' words and hoped she would not be a disappointment to this warm, loving Texas family.

"This calls for a toast," Pops boomed.

The four circled the dining room table, as Pops poured champagne into their upraised glasses.

"What about a ring, son?"

Chip reddened. "I haven't quite planned that yet," he admitted. "It just sort of happened."

Dorothy scurried into her bedroom and returned with a folded handkerchief.

"Robert, I've been saving this for you, and it looks like I was right to do so. Here," she said unfolding the lace-edged cloth. "I gave up wearing this a long time ago."

Mrs. Stephens emptied the contents into Chip's open palm. A delicate, white-gold filigree band wound around a diamond that flashed in the dining room light.

"It belonged to Mitchell's mother," Dorothy explained. "And now it should belong to you."

Dorothy hugged the young woman, then stepped aside as Chip faced his fiancée.

Chip reached for Angela's hand and brought the ring to her finger. "My darling, you've made me the happiest man alive."

Angela couldn't repress the smile that grew from the inside out. "I love you," she whispered.

Sunday afternoons proved to be lazy for the whole Stephens clan. It was close to noon when Dorothy and Pops returned from church and served brunch. Afterward, Pops and Chip fed the livestock while Mrs. Stephens puttered in her garden.

Angela finished packing her overnight bag and zipped it closed. The noise from an approaching car caught her attention. Angela peered out the window and watched as a young man driving an older Camaro roared up to the house, raising a roostertail of dust behind him. Jasper raced to the driver's side, barking and leaping excitedly. A dark-haired young man emerged from the car and rumpled the dog's fur. He strode up the steps to the porch and yanked the screen door open.

"Hey, anybody ho—"

Angela met him in the living room and smiled. "You must be Bobby Ray."

"Yes, ma'am."

"Angela," she said, extending her hand.

Bobby Ray glanced at her, and his gaze drifted to the ring on her left hand. "Hi."

It was obvious by his reticence that Bobby Ray's personality and that of his father's were on opposite ends of the spectrum. Angela ignored his cool study of her and dropped her hand.

"How was your trip?"

"It was okay."

"Your father tells me you're graduating this year . . ."

"Listen, I've got to go clean up. Would you excuse me?"

The young man didn't wait for an answer, but vacated the room as quickly as he had entered it.

Dorothy came into the house wiping garden dirt from her hands. "Was that Bobby Ray?"

"He went to clean up." *And hopes I'm gone when he gets back.*

"He's back already? Robert will be pleased. We were afraid you'd miss meeting him."

Angela smiled weakly.

Dorothy had prepared a light meal before their departure. Pops returned from the barn in high spirits. "We better eat and get these two on their way," he announced, slamming his hat on the table.

"I've got a little something ready." Dorothy eyed a trail of mud that began at the back door. "Mitchell, did you track that in here?"

Pops peered down at his boots and eyed the trail that he had left from the patio door. " 'Fraid so, Dorie. Let me just mosey on out of here—" The tall man tip-toed to the back door and closed it behind him.

"Gracious, these boys never do grow up, do they?" Dorothy had already manned a broom and followed Pops' muddy path to the back door where she met her son. "Robert, you remove those boots before you traipse in here, now."

Chip obediently complied and removed his boots before he entered.

"Did I see Bobby Ray drive in?"

"Uh-huh." Angela nodded.

"You met him, then?"

"You could say that."

"Real talkative, right?"

Angela raised a questioning brow. "I wouldn't call him talkative. He scooted out of here as fast as he could."

"I'll speak to him."

"No," Angela cautioned. "He's all right. I'd leave it alone."

Chip shook his head. "I'd like very much for you two to become friends."

"That may take time, Chip. I'm sure he's not comfortable having another woman in the house."

"He just doesn't know you yet, honey. He's going to

love you just like I do." Chip circled his arms around her waist and pulled her close. "We can't spend too much time here. We've got that five-thirty flight."

Angela hated their visit to end. "I'm ready when you are."

The teenager cloistered himself in the bathroom until the hot water had apparently run out. He emerged, rakish, handsome, hair wet, teasing the collar of his lightweight cowboy shirt.

"Dinner's on, son," Chip coaxed. "Sit down and eat with us."

"I ate in town."

"Then sit and visit with us," Dorothy instructed. "Angela and your father will be leaving soon.

Bobby Ray dropped into a chair next to Pops and averted his gaze.

"How was your trip, boy?" Pops asked.

"Good, sir."

"You all got back in good time," Dorothy added.

"Yes'm."

"Your father has something to tell you." Dorothy smiled and nodded at Chip.

"Bobby Ray, I wanted you to meet Miss Angela Lawrey. I've proposed, and we're going to be married."

The silence was awkward for Angela, but Pops and Dorothy seemed not to notice. "Isn't it wonderful?" Dorothy asked the young man. "I imagine we'll have the wedding here, won't we, Robert?"

"Of course we will," Pops interrupted. "Angel's going to bring her folks down, aren't you?"

"Well, I—" Angela hedged.

"We haven't decided just yet." Chip circled his arm

around Angela's shoulders. "We'll have to work out those details later."

"How much later? I'll have to work around my crops, and Bobby Ray's graduation—"

"I'm pretty tired." The young man stood and backed from his chair. "Do you mind if I go on upstairs?"

"But your father—" Dorie stopped when she caught Pop's glance. "Of course, Bobby Ray. You're excused."

"I'll be up to see you before I leave," Chip told him.

"Miss Lawrey." Bobby Ray nodded his head curtly and quickly exited the room.

"He's going to the barn?"

"He bunks above the tack room," Chip explained.

Dorothy shook her head. "I don't know what's got into him. He's usually much more sociable, Angela. I guess he must be tired."

Angela nodded. "I'm sure he is. Don't worry. I remember what it was like—being a teenager."

After supper, Chip loaded their bags into the car. Angela visited with Dorothy in the kitchen, while Pops and Chip headed for the barn. A short time later, Chip returned, looking a little disgruntled.

"Problems?" Angela asked.

"Ah, Bobby Ray's got a stubborn streak. I asked him to come say goodbye, but he won't budge. I'm sorry, Angel."

"Let me talk to him," she suggested. "It's hard for a young man to be hit with news like that. Maybe I can reach him."

Chip grinned. "Honey, you're welcome to try." He kissed the tip of her nose. "I'll wait for you inside, but we can't be too long."

"I know. I'll be just a minute."

Angela climbed the rough wooden stairway that looked as

if it were an afterthought to the tack room. She knocked on the trap door and waited until Chip's son yelled, "It's open."

Angela pushed open the trap door and climbed the remaining stairs into the hideaway room. A television and stereo were stacked on an entertainment center next to a student-sized desk. Behind the door, the youth lounged on a futon. Dressed in jeans, a white T-shirt and cowboy boots, he looked every bit the young Texas rancher.

"Nice room." Angela fingered a pair of antique spurs that hung by leather bindings. "Grandpa Rose's?"

"Texas Vaquero." He corrected. "Did you come to say goodbye?"

"Yes." She paused. "And I thought I'd visit for a minute, if you didn't mind."

"Suit yourself." He nodded in the direction of a bean bag that slouched in the corner of the room.

Angela sank into the voluminous bag and tried to position herself to maintain eye contact.

"So you're going to marry my dad?"

"We haven't worked out the details yet."

"Going to live in Colorado?"

"We just got engaged last night. We haven't really planned—"

The young man shrugged and tried to look like none of this mattered. Angela felt as if she had entered a lion's cage without chair or whip.

"They told you my mother died?"

"Yes. Chip told me. My mom left me and my dad a long time ago," she added, "I know what that's like."

"Yeah? Did she leave you an orphan?"

"No. I had my dad."

"Hmmph. I guess you could say I did too."

"You had your grandmother, and Pops."

"What are you? A social worker or something?"

"Air traffic controller."

"So what's this got to do with me?"

"I was just hoping maybe we could be friendly . . . if not friends."

"Sure. Whatever you say."

Angela felt frustrated by his animosity. "Is there something about me that you don't like? Something maybe you disapprove of?"

He glared at her, the look on his face shadowed by anger. "I don't need a mother," he retorted. "I had one."

"I know, Bobby Ray. I wouldn't replace her. I know that."

"I don't suppose anyone showed you this." He thrust a small framed picture at her and allowed Angela to take it from his hand.

Angela's eyes widened then narrowed as she studied the smiling face of a dark-haired young woman. If Angela had been a twin, she was looking at her sister. The color photo had faded slightly over time, but the dark hair and green eyes could have passed for her own. The heart-shaped face and wide smile were that of a young woman in love. It may as well be her.

"I think it's kind of funny that you look alike. Don't you?"

Angela couldn't respond. The likeness was uncanny.

"Who'd you say he was marrying?" He demanded. "You? Or my mother?"

Angela had seen and heard all she cared to. She laid the picture on the futon and with as much decorum as she could muster, unwound herself from the bean bag and stood. "I didn't mean to upset you," she sighed. "I'll see you later." Angela started down the stairway.

"Yeah. Later," Bobby Ray repeated.

Angela left the shaded barn and squinted in the bright sunlight. A hawk shrieked in the tall branches of the large oak near the house. She looked up, but couldn't see the bird. Paint whinnied from the corral and Angela wandered over to where the mare stood.

"You gonna miss me, girl?" She stroked the horse's muzzle.

"We're all gonna miss you, Angel." Pops appeared at the edge of the corral and joined her. "You'll be comin' back for Bobby Ray's graduation, won't you?"

Angela hesitated. "I'll see what I can do."

"That doesn't sound too certain to me," Pops deduced. "How about a for-sure?"

Angela glanced at Chip and Dorothy talking by the car. Although her encounter with Bobby Ray was far from satisfactory, Angela thought better of refusing the old man.

"I promise."

"Good. We'll look forward to it." Pops circled his arm about her and walked her to the car. "Don't let the grass grow under your feet, now. You're part of our family, and we want you back as soon as you can. I'll have Paint ready for you to ride."

Angela felt a heaviness tugging at her heart. It was a familiar ache, but it pushed her close to tears. Something deep weighed heavy in her soul and made her feel she didn't belong . . . as if she wasn't worthy of the happiness Chip and his family offered. When they reached the car, she hugged the elder Stephens.

"Good-bye, Pops."

"So long, for now," he corrected her. "We don't need to say good-bye."

Dorothy kissed her son then hugged Angela good-bye.

She and Pops stood side by side, waving as Chip pulled away.

Chip wasn't as talkative on the return trip as he had been the day before. Angela hoped it was because he was tired. She didn't want to ask about his former wife in the public environment of airport, airplane or taxi. In truth, she didn't want to bring it up at all. It would have to wait.

Only when they deplaned at DIA, did he embrace her like a man who was leaving his fiancée. "We'll talk soon, Angel. We've got lots of plans to make."

Angela studied the lines around his eyes. "Take it slow, Chip," she cautioned. "Let's get through the graduation before we start making plans, shall we?"

"But, Angel, we've got to get started. If we need to consult your parents—"

"We don't need to involve them at this point," she countered. "And besides, we need to let Bobby Ray get used to this before we impose a stranger into his life."

Chip looked crestfallen. "Honey, I want you in my life as soon as possible. We've been apart too long already."

"I didn't want to say anything, but I think we need to talk."

"About what?"

"Bobby Ray's mother."

Chip jerked backward as if he'd been slapped. "What about her?"

"I saw her picture." Angela forced the breath from her lungs and looked him squarely in the face. "You didn't tell me we looked so alike."

The muscle in Chip's jaw tightened visibly and he looked wounded. "There's a resemblance," he admitted.

"You didn't tell me."

"I didn't think it mattered. Angel, when I saw you that day, all I could think about was you. I can't explain it."

"You don't think you were trying to recreate your relationship with Rayanne?" she challenged. "Didn't it occur to you that you may have been looking for *her* all this time?"

"No! I love you and I won't have you, or Bobby Ray, making this into anything else."

"But Chip, isn't it possible?"

He shifted his overnight bag on his shoulder and checked his watch. "Honey, I'm sorry. I can't discuss this right now. I have to catch that flight to L.A."

"But, Chip—"

"I'll call you when I get home."

Angela shook her head. "I've got the early shift."

"Then I'll call you tomorrow—or the next day. Tell me when." Chip was walking backwards now.

"I'll leave a message," she murmured.

"What?"

"I'll call you," she shouted.

"I love you, honey." He waved and turned away. She watched as he jogged down the concourse, weaving between people like a running back dodging a tackle.

Angela usually arrived before Richie, and today was no exception. She clocked in for the early morning shift and walked into the control room that buzzed like a bee hive. All of the controllers seemed agitated she noticed as she neared her station.

"What's going on, Davis?" she asked the young man she was to relieve.

"UFO's. All over the place."

"What?" She leaned over his shoulder and scanned his

monitor. Numerous unidentified targets on the screen zigged-zagged over and around similar live traffic. She peered at the station next to hers and noticed that that monitor had the same traffic.

"UFO's? Are these confirmed targets?"

"It's been going on about twenty minutes." Davis sounded grave. "We think it's a result of the Grand Junction power failure yesterday."

"I hadn't heard."

"We've got several sectors affected," Davis informed her. "They're phantom targets that look like aircraft."

"Traveling at the same speed and altitudes." She observed.

"Yep. Next to impossible to figure what's real and what's not."

"Oh, boy." She sighed.

Sam Rankin joined Angela behind Davis. "You ready, Lawrey?"

"Ready as I'll ever be, I guess." Angela settled herself in the seat next to Davis. Donning her headphones, Angela took over.

The UFO's had disappeared by ten o'clock. Tension had mounted throughout the center, and a mandatory break-out meeting was scheduled for early Tuesday morning. Angela and Richie found seats before Haskell and two upper-management speakers arrived.

Haskell cleared his throat and rapped on the podium for attention. He began the meeting by introducing the Center's safety chairman. Reading from a written statement, the chairman tried to explain the outage they believed was responsible for the erroneous targets. When he had finished, Haskell took the microphone.

"As Phil explained, regional managers are convinced the problem lay with the transponders."

A unilateral groan arose from his audience. "Blame it on anything but our computers," someone muttered. "How did the outage affect our ability to read targets?" another asked.

"Settle down," he warned. "I know you don't like to hear that, but to be absolutely sure, we have to test the computer."

"Test? Test? We don't need no stinking test," someone joked.

"We're scheduling it for the lightest hours of traffic," Haskell continued. "Between nine p.m. and three a.m."

"Six hours?" someone from the audience demanded. "That's too long."

"It'll wreak havoc," another shouted.

A volley of affirmations supported those who spoke up.

"Long enough to crash a few airplanes," Richie whispered. "Pretty poor timing if you ask me."

"They didn't ask." Angela shifted in her metal folding chair, hoping to ease her saddle-induced ache. She hadn't felt it at the time, but Monday morning came with the realization that she had muscles in places she had forgotten about. She cocked her head, trying to listen.

"I know it's going to be hectic and confusing, but those of you on the swing shift will have to manage. It is not, I repeat, not unsafe. It *will* be challenging, however," Haskell argued.

Several more hands flew upward and others voiced their opinions without the benefit of courtesy.

"We were supposed to have that equipment operational three years ago," someone complained. "FAA scrapped the contract for new equipment because it wasn't compatible with the system we're supposed to have. If the media gets hold of this—"

Haskell and his supervisor downplayed their concerns. This computer test would be another step to ensure passenger safety and its conclusions should prove that theory.

The safety chairman again took the podium. "The bottom line is, the head of the safety committee for the controller's union believes that the computer went haywire following the outage. What we need to determine is if it was coincidence or a direct result of the outage."

After a few minutes they adjourned the meeting and the controllers were dismissed.

"So," Richie leaned into Angela's shoulder. "What's your schedule? Are you on that shift?"

"Thankfully, no." She sighed. "I'm on days for the next two weeks."

"Me too. They know not to split up a good partnership." Richie grinned. "Can I have your dessert today?"

"Be my guest." Angela rose and smoothed her skirt.

They left the upstairs meeting room and headed for the lounge before their shift was scheduled to start.

"So, Ang . . . how are you?"

"Miserable," she muttered.

"What d'ya mean? I thought you went to meet the folks. Didn't it go well?"

Angela sighed. "Not now, Richie. I can't think straight. Okay?"

"Sure. I didn't mean to—"

"It's not you. You know that."

"Yeah. I know. Man! Everybody is so touchy these days."

Angela looked at her partner and gave him a half-hearted smile. "I'm engaged."

"You're *what?*"

"I'm engaged," she repeated.

Richie lifted her left hand and angled his head. "I see. Pretty nice rock there, missy."

Angela withdrew her hand. "It's not a rock. It's an heirloom."

"So tell me," he coaxed. "Why the long face? It looks like the trip went well. What's up?"

Angela sighed and averted his questioning gaze. "He has a son."

"Already? Good grief, you two work fast."

"Not me. Chip. He's seventeen. Almost out of high school."

"That's a problem? He'll be out of the nest before you know it. Of course, you may have to help foot the college bill, but, hey—"

"It's not that," she paused. "He lost his mother when he was a baby and I was told, unequivocally, that he doesn't want a replacement."

"At seventeen? Can't say I'd feel any different. Who needs a mother?"

Angela faced him raising a brow.

"No offense, of course," he added.

"You're incorrigible, Richie."

"Hey, don't let the kid thing get you down. He's outta there before you know it, and you'll have Southern Comfort all to yourself."

"His name is Chip."

"Good name, Chip," Richie repeated. "Easy to spell. Will look great on your reception napkins." Richie nudged her and winked.

"You'll come to the wedding, won't you, Richie?"

"Of course, I'll come. I'll be your best man."

"You are wonderful, you know that?"

"Aw shucks, ma'am," Richie drawled. "Don't make me blush."

"Come on, you clown." Angela pushed back her chair. "Let's get to work. We've got a few planes to round up."

Angela left two messages on Chip's answering machine that week, and he left one on hers saying he would call her Saturday. Angela worried about their follow-up conversation. It was silly of her to think that Chip was avoiding the discussion when he just had to catch that L.A. flight. But it bothered her, just the same.

Saturday came and Angela kept herself busy cleaning her condominium, running errands and grocery shopping. It was afternoon before she finished her chores.

Later, she spent time swimming laps in the pool. When she returned from her workout, a blinking light on her answering machine indicated a message had been left.

Angela blotted her hair while she listened. It was Chip. "Sorry I missed you, Angel. I've got meetings in Denver two nights this week. I'll call you in between." He affectionately ended the call with, "Over."

She smiled. Turning her hand at different angles, she studied the ring on her finger. The small diamond glittered and brought to mind the night at the Stephens' ranch. *Apparently my resemblance to Chip's former wife hadn't been a concern to either Dorothy or Pops. Why should I make such an issue of it?*

Angela sank into her couch and picked up the local paper. Beneath the headlines a secondary column blared, "Another Near Miss!" The reporter cited the computer problems they had experienced that week, in addition to the test that was supposed to have been confidential. Shocked, Angela continued to read. *An unnamed source confirmed that several operational errors had occurred while the computers were down. An operational error is committed when two planes have flown closer than one thousand feet vertical separation and five miles horizontal.*

The Denver paper had also picked up the story. Angela slammed down the newspaper, feeling strong emotions of betrayal and anger. *Who would tear down their reputation and morale? How far will they go to undermine the entire structure?* She felt tired and, for the first time in her air traffic career, dreaded Monday morning. *Will this nightmare ever end?*

Chapter Nine

"Did you see those clouds out there?" Richie asked Angela as he settled into the data position seat beside her station.

"Gargantuan cumulonimbus," Angela stated. "I'll bet there's some low-level wind shear in that." Angela narrowed her gaze to the screen. "I saw them earlier."

"Radio said that there was a heck of a storm building in the southeast. Any problems at DIA?"

"Not so far."

"I know I'm supposed to log in," Richie said. "But can you give me a minute?"

"Sure."

Richie turned away, apple in hand. "I'll be right back."

Angela took a call from the Utah controller handing over a flight. She watched the blip from the left side of her screen. "Transway 155, this is Denver Center, do you copy?"

"Denver Center, this is Transway 155 at flight level three zero zero."

"Roger One Five Five. Continue on course, level three zero zero."

"Denver Center, this is Transway 155. We've encountered clear air turbulence. Had a ninety knot change here. Are there—whoa!"

"Transway 155, Denver Center. Repeat."

"Any reports of wind shear? We're experiencing some turbulence here."

"We've had no reports in this sector."

Angela felt herself tense. Transway 155 was a large commuter originating in San Francisco. Several seconds passed with no word from the pilot.

Suddenly, her headphones filled with static. "Denver Center, it's a little hard to hold," he said. "Unusual cloud patterns on the port side."

Angela noted the time. Ten twenty nine and twenty five seconds.

"Another eighty knot gain." The pilot cursed. "Unusual turbulence. Suspect wind rotor."

Angela held her breath. Her training had included a section on wind rotor—winds defined as horizontal tornadoes. She remembered the class had included the cockpit recording of a big craft like the 155 before it crashed. The similarity in wind speed, weather conditions and location terrified her. She had no personal experience with wind rotor. A morbid fear gripped her. She felt her heart rate increase and her palms on the keyboard moistened. *What can I do?*

"Transway 155, Denver Center. Maintain altitude."

Her instructions were heeled by the pilot's uncensored

expletive. "Denver Center, four thousand foot altitude drop. Request heading to clear turbulence."

At that moment Richie returned to her station. "Get the area supervisor," Angela ordered.

"Transway 155, Denver Center. What is your altitude and speed?"

"Altitude two-five-nine. Speed two-five-zero."

"Increase speed to three-zero-zero. Climb to thirty thousand." *Try to get on top of it*, she prayed.

"Denver Center, copy."

Haskell and Richie closed in on either side of her. Although she needed them nearby, their presence seemed cloying. She struggled to breathe.

"Transway 155, did you copy?"

"Roger. Assumed three-zero-zero. Altitude thirty thousand."

She strained to listen to the one-sided cockpit conversation as the pilot conferred with his copilot. "Never did fly over the Rockies this time of year without getting sick. Flaky weather." She heard him say.

"Transway 155, Denver Center. What is your status?"

"We seem to be skirting the edge of something here. Maintaining speed. Leveling at two-eight-zero."

Angela released her breath. She glanced up at Haskell. "Got a possible wind rotor, Bob. I sent him up to thirty three thousand and—"

"Denver Center, Transway 155, picked up two hundred knot air speed. Can't control."

Angela froze. Her breathing halted as she listened to the captain's panicked voice as he desperately tried to regain control of the craft.

"Oh, God!" The pilot shouted into her headphones. Then all was silent, as if their line had been cut.

"What's going on?" Haskell demanded.

Angela's eyes remained fixed on the screen as the blip disappeared.

"Lawrey!" Haskell bellowed. Angela felt the blood drain from her face. Her hands fell limp and slipped off the keyboard.

"We've got a situation!" She heard him roar. "Give me a hand over here."

Sam Rankin and another controller hustled to Angela's station and tried to ease her from her chair.

"No." She resisted. "I'm stay—"

"Get her to medical, Richie," Haskell barked. "Rankin, take over."

"Bob!" Angela pleaded. "Let me—" She shrank from Haskell. He was in charge and she was dismissed. Angela allowed the men to help her from her chair. She felt as lifeless as the rag doll she used to play with as a child.

Rankin grabbed the second set of headphones and took over. "Transway 155, this is Denver Center, copy?" He shook his head. "Nothing, Bob."

"Try again," Haskell demanded. "For God's sake!"

Rankin tried again to contact the craft but it was evident they could no longer respond.

Her coworkers struggled to hold onto her as they guided her toward the medical clinic in the building. She couldn't fully comprehend that she had gone into shock. She was only aware of the dazed feeling that left her emotionally and physically numb.

"I lost them."

"You'll be all right," Richie said.

"I think they crashed." She heard herself say.

Richie pushed open the clinic door and held it while the other man led her inside.

"What have we got here?" the nurse asked.

Angela allowed herself to be led into the examining room. She was aware of low voices talking behind the closed door.

"I tried—"

Richie hushed her. "You'll be okay, Ang. The doctor will be right in."

Tears eased down her face. They felt warm and tasted salty on her lips. She blinked her eyes and waited for the room to stop spinning. Then everything went black.

When she woke, the doctor's face swam hazily in front of her. She was aware of the nurse, monitoring her blood pressure. Richie stood close by.

"She's coming 'round," she heard the doctor say. "Can you hear me, Ms. Lawrey?"

Angela peered beyond the doctor to the dark, deadly sky outside. It was as gloomy and gray as her disturbed state of mind. Tears distorted her view, as she sought Richie's gaze. "They're all dead, aren't they?"

"We don't have the details," he soothed. "Don't think about it now."

"Oh, Richie. What happened?"

"We're not sure, Ang. Don't say anything, okay?" He gently picked up her limp hand and held it, avoiding the intravenous syringe.

"I blacked out?" She lifted her bandaged hand. "What's this?"

"Sugar water," the nurse responded. "The ambulance will be here shortly."

"Ambulance? But I'm on duty," she argued. "I have to get back."

"We can't treat you here, and we can't presume the cause of your blackout," the doctor stated.

"Are you pregnant?" the nurse asked.

"No!"

"Diabetic?"

Angela's lips trembled. "No." She shook her head. "Don't you understand? I lost an aircraft! I didn't mean to—"

Richie hushed her. "It's okay, Ang. It's okay."

"It's not okay. It'll never be okay." She sobbed. "Richie, I can't go out of here in an ambulance!"

"It's procedure, miss," the doctor explained. "They'll run tests at the hospital."

"I don't need tests. I must have fainted, that's all." Desperate, she grabbed Richie's hand. "Richie, tell Haskell—"

"Haskell knows, Ang. He asked me to go with you."

"But my shift—"

"We've got that covered."

Haskell's supervisor knocked on the door and entered the room flanked by two blue-uniformed paramedics. The gurney they rolled in looked ominous as they began releasing the safety straps that would hold her.

"I don't need that," she protested.

"Miss Lawrey, Mr. Lange will accompany you to the hospital. I'll arrange for my assistant to drive you home from there. It's procedure following this kind of situation."

"But I'm all right. I should get back to work."

"You're relieved until further notice. We won't discuss this now. I've released you to these attendants. The hospital will run tests—"

"I don't need any tests! Please—"

"I'll go with you," Richie interrupted. "Don't argue."

Richie's voice assumed a tone Angela wasn't used to. She noted the seriousness in his eyes and pondered her predicament.

"I'll go home," she whispered. "But I'm walking out."

The paramedics met the gaze of the facility doctor who nodded.

"Let me get my purse."

"I'll get it, Miss Lawrey," the nurse volunteered. "Do you have your locker key?"

Angela tugged a key ring from her pocket and handed it to her. "Seven one four."

The paramedics wheeled the gurney out the doors and down the hall toward the entrance.

"We'll be right with you," Richie assured them. "C'mon, Ang. Take my arm."

Angela felt as small and helpless as a child. Embarrassed, she hated walking past her coworkers, who looked to be in the midst of the turmoil and stress that followed the accident. She wished she could disappear.

After several hours of tests and intense counseling, Angela was released. Feeling like a prisoner who had posted bail, she and Richie were picked up by the director's assistant.

"You're on administrative leave for the remainder of the week. When you return, you'll be required to attend a mandatory training course before you're allowed to return to the floor."

"Is that something like being guilty before you're proven innocent?" she muttered.

"Protocol."

"Kind of like no-fault insurance," Richie suggested, turning to the aid. "Right?"

"No guilt or innocence presumed. It doesn't matter what the incident; it's routine."

In an instant, her career had changed from a promising future to a black, bottomless void. She couldn't imagine how it would ever return to normal again.

"We advise you to have someone stay with you the rest of this week. I understand you live alone?"

Angela nodded.

"Are there relatives, or a close friend you can stay with?"

Her senses dulled, a distorted image of Chip wafted in her head then disappeared. As much as she believed she was in love with the pilot, he had his own life and obligations. She didn't dare throw her troubles at him—they were barely engaged. There was no one else in her life she could turn to. Angela shook her head. Her throat ached and burned. The pain was matched only by the heaviness in her heart. "No one," she croaked.

"Someone will have to be available to you on a twenty four hour basis. You understand that, Ms. Lawrey?"

Angela closed her eyes and nodded. She wanted no one near her on the heels of this unimaginable terror. She did not believe she could live with the shame of this day.

"I'll stay with her," Richie blurted. "I'll see that she's not alone."

"But, Richie—"

"Don't argue, Ang. I'll get my things and come over."

She turned her head and stared, unseeing. It was small comfort that someone cared enough to try to help. She would never ask for it, but she didn't have the strength to argue. Having an unrelated male in her home was a direct violation of the ethics code Haskell had warned her about. But the last thing she considered at this moment was her reputation.

The therapist recommended a sedative to calm her. She took one, as ordered, while still in the hospital. By the time they arrived at her home, it seemed to have taken effect. She felt a little light-headed and unsure of her footing. Richie walked her to the door and unlocked it for her.

"What about my car?"

"Want me to bring it?" Richie asked.

She handed her keys to him.

"I'll drive it back with my things. I'll be here in about an hour."

Angela nodded and walked inside. She felt a throbbing in the back of her neck that surged upward into a horrendous headache. She couldn't control her involuntary reaction to the post-traumatic stress. The doctor had prescribed several kinds of medication for her anxiety and trauma: anti-depressants, sleep-inducing pills, pills with names she could not pronounce, pills she didn't want. Even during the ride home, Angela felt as if she were trapped in a vacuum where emotions, physical senses and simple human responses were unmanageable.

She thought it was dawn and the alarm was rousing her, but when she forced her eyes open, the clock read half past six. It was not the alarm, but the telephone ringing. By the time she reached the handset beside her bed, the answering machine had picked up the call and she heard her voice from the living room instructing the caller to leave a message.

It was Chip. "I heard Denver had some sorrowful news today, darlin'. I'm guessing you might still be on the job, so I won't talk long. I'll phone again this week when things have calmed down a bit."

The accident must have made national news, since Chip

was phoning from Los Angeles. *It was me,* she wanted to scream. *I was responsible!* The guilt she felt increased her depression. She curled into a tight ball on her large bed and sobbed.

The doorbell rang and rang, then rang again. Angela hoped whoever it was would leave. She heard the door opening, then thought she recognized Richie's voice.

"Ang? Are you okay? It's me, Richie." She pushed herself from her bed and met Richie at the front door.

"I'm sorry to bust in on you."

"It's okay," she croaked. "I was just getting up."

Richie looked as tired and forlorn as she had ever seen him.

"You look terrible," she managed to say.

"Then I'm in good company. You don't look so hot yourself."

Angela caught her trembling lip between her teeth. It was difficult not to cry.

"Have you eaten?" he ventured.

"No."

"I don't want to be pushy, Ang. But you've got to eat something."

"Richie. I know you want to help. But don't. I can't face you. I can't face anyone right now."

"I know, trooper. But I brought you some soup, anyway. You've got to have something in your stomach. I saw that bag full of pills the doctor gave you. You're going to have to keep your strength up."

"But—"

"It's Thai," he baited. "Your favorite."

"I don't want it."

Richie hung his head. "Gee. I know my cooking is bad, but—"

"I can't ask you to stay Richie. It isn't right."

"Well," Richie soothed. "It's me or someone else. "If you really don't want me here—"

She lifted her head and dragged the back of her hand across her eyes. She gulped hard, trying to swallow that ball of pain in her throat. She shook her head. "The guest bedroom is down the hall."

"Does it have a TV?"

"No."

"Then I'll sleep in the living room. You've got a big screen out there."

Angela sniffed and managed to gain control of herself. She nodded. "Okay."

She watched dully as he retreated to her car, then returned with his bags. "Here are your keys," he said, handing the dainty keychain to her.

"You're too good to me, Rich."

"I know. But you're going to make it up to me. I keep track of my IOU's."

Richie deposited the local paper onto her coffee table. "Thought you might want to see this."

Angela gasped when she saw the headline, *"Hundreds Die in Colorado Air Disaster."*

Richie snatched it from her hand. "Maybe I shouldn't have."

Angela hung her head. "It's okay. I'm glad you did."

Richie shoved it into his opened duffel bag.

"Later." He threw his hands together and rubbed them vigorously, surveying the living room. "So. Let's eat."

The evening news confirmed that it had been one of the deadliest air disasters in Colorado's history. All of the crew and passengers on Transway Flight 155 perished in the Colorado prairie that morning. The cockpit recorder, if it could be found, might provide more conclusive evidence, but it seemed that the plane had flown into an extreme rotor wind before it bored into the ground at the instructed speed of three hundred miles per hour.

Instructed speed. The words almost screamed at her. *Controller error.* It was said that a controller had been suspended with pay pending an investigation.

The director's assistant had advised her that the FAA would provide a defense attorney. It could be a long, drawn-out investigation and the trial may be delayed up to six months, pending evidence.

The nurse at the Center had arranged for a volunteer to sit with Angela during the day. The woman was available but not intrusive, occupying herself in the living room with her favorite soap operas and a crochet project. After Angela had rested overnight, she felt fully alert and anxious to leave her confinement. She wanted to run as far and as fast from Longmont as she could, and forget it ever happened. She couldn't, though. She knew she'd never forget the unpredictable Colorado weather and the accident that took so many lives. In a way, it had taken hers.

Several times over the next few days, Angela picked up the handset to make a call. She dialed Chip's number. She wanted badly to speak with him, but when she heard his voice on the recorder, she replaced the handset. Pride and humiliation weakened her, driving her thoughts deeper into herself. *What would Chip think of me now? How could he possibly want to entangle himself with a woman of dubious career and credentials?* Her whole world had plummeted along with that plane.

The kindly woman who introduced herself as Maggie brought Angela water, tea and a light lunch for her around noon. Angela stayed in her room for several hours. She ventured out once to use the clubhouse sauna and pool, but didn't leave again. Although she never saw anyone, she felt as if she were being watched. *Had the paper named names? Did her neighbors, the whole town, even her parents know that she was the controller in charge of that fatal crash?* When Richie returned from his shift that afternoon, Maggie left.

By Thursday evening, Richie seemed to be perfectly relaxed in her home. He had taken over the guest bathroom, laundry room, kitchen and living room as his domain. It was becoming obvious that a man lived in her house. Shorts, socks and shaving equipment adorned the guest bathroom. Richie was like the younger brother she never had. He was singularly cheerful, oblivious to his messiness, and playful in his approach.

Like many men, Richie liked action movies. He had rented half a dozen by the time he had spent four evenings in her home. Angela was soaking in her tub one night when she thought she heard the telephone ring, though she couldn't be sure over the noise of the video.

After she had finished her bath, she wandered out to the living room and found Richie sprawled in front of the TV, his large feet propped on her glass coffee table.

"Hey, Ang. Come join me. This is good."

"No thanks. I'm going to have some tea and go back to my room. Do you want anything?"

Richie dipped his hand into a super-sized bag of chips. "Nah, I'm covered. Hey, your pilot friend called."

"Chip?"

"Yeah. Your fiancé."

Angela's heart jolted. "What did he say? I mean—what did you say?"

"I told him you were relaxing. He didn't sound too pleased. Didn't you tell him?"

"Oh, Richie . . ."

Angela's heart raced. *What will Chip think—Richie answering her phone?* She waited impatiently as Chip's number rang and rang again. *Come on, Chip,* she prayed.

The phone clicked and Chip answered. "Hello?"

"Chip, it's Angela."

"Angel? What in blue blazes is goin' on over there? I've been trying to call you all week."

"I know. I haven't been answering the phone."

"Why not? You know I've been trying to reach you. I even left a message at the Center."

Angela felt her stomach sink. "You called my job?"

"I know I shouldn't have, honey, but I couldn't reach you and I got worried."

Angela responded to his comment with silence and felt an uncomfortable tension growing between them.

"Angela?"

She clutched the phone that was pressed tight against her ear. "Yes?"

"Does this have anything to do with—"

"What?"

"That man in your house?"

Angela closed her eyes and clenched the phone. "Are you suggesting . . . ?"

"No, honey, of course not, it's just that—I don't know what's going on. I don't know what I'm supposed to think."

Angela felt her jaw tighten. "I don't want to talk to anyone right now. I've got some things I need to work out and I'll work them out alone."

"But—"

"I've got to go."

"But—"

"I'll be in touch when I can."

"Angel, you don't sound like yourself."

"I've got to go, Chip. I'll call you later."

"When?"

"Next week."

"Next week? But I'll be in Denver over the weekend."

"I'm going to be busy." She hedged.

"But—"

"Goodbye, Chip." Angela replaced the handset, sat down on the edge of her bed and covered her face with her hands. She felt like a prisoner in her own home—not allowed to be left alone for a minute. For all she knew her phone could be tapped. Her emotions were spinning out of control. She had been too harsh to Chip, ungrateful to Richie, and resentful of the nurse. She just wanted to be left alone!

She desperately wanted to fall asleep, but her mind wouldn't let her. She turned her head and stared, unseeing, at the wall. Finally, giving in to her quiet desperation, Angela took another pill. At about 3:30 A.M. she left her tortured world and slipped into a dream.

When she awoke on Friday, Richie had been gone for hours and the volunteer had arrived. She had slept through half of the day. Feeling drugged, she forced herself from her bed and into a hot shower. She had an appointment with both her counselor and the F.A.A. doctor. If they cleared her she would return to work on Monday. She dressed in a blue twill double-breasted suit, red silk blouse and heels. Angela knew she looked good, but emotionally, she was still a little hesitant. She felt like she had been thrown by a horse and was forcing herself to get back in the saddle. She wanted to return to work, so, ready or not, she planned to make it happen.

Her session with the counselor proved grueling at best, emotionally draining at the worst. After visiting with the physician, however, it was determined that she was ready to return to work. She had passed the danger period and was officially released from house-watch. The volunteer nurse was dismissed and Angela was scheduled to report to work Monday for a refresher training course. Now all that remained was for Richie to move out.

On Saturday morning, Angela convinced Richie that his services as night watchman were no longer needed. After a late breakfast, Angela helped Richie pack and load his car. It was a cool spring day, bright with sunshine in a cloudless sky—a world away from the storm that had changed her life only a few short days ago.

"I don't know why you're in such a hurry to get rid of me," Richie complained. "I was beginning to get used to this condo-life."

"You need a keeper, Richie. I don't." Angela shoved a bulging canvas laundry bag onto the backseat of his foreign car. "I've never seen anyone accumulate so much dirty laundry in a four-day period."

"That was a week's worth. I brought all my laundry over."

"That explains it." Angela closed the car door and brushed the dust from his vehicle onto her jeans.

"Too bad you don't have a car wash in your community. I could use it."

Angela planted her hands on her hips and peered at him over the top of his car. "I owe you, Richie."

"Yep. I'll collect someday. If I happen to catch that cold that's going around, I expect chicken soup," he said, grinning.

"Dumplings?"

"Egg noodles. The way grandma used to make it."

At that moment a Lincoln Towncar swerved into her driveway. She and Richie both looked at the driver, who wore a military-looking uniform. Angela gasped. "Oh my gosh. It's Chip."

"Chip? Your pilot, Chip? What's he doing here?"

Angela felt her face flame. "Get going, Richie, will you?"

"You don't want to introduce—"

"Richie!" Angela pleaded.

"All right, all right." Richie slid his lanky frame behind the small steering wheel, and slammed the driver's door. "I'm going." He twisted his key into the ignition. After a series of whirring, the starter caught and the little engine revved.

Captain Stephens emerged from his car and watched as Richie spun the car into a wide U-turn and peeled out.

Chapter Ten

Angela's heartbeat accelerated as Chip drew near. A mixture of longing, fear and dread tumbled in her chest. He wasn't smiling.

"Who was that?" Chip looked confused. His brow furrowed uncharacteristically, and he searched her face for answers.

"Richie."

"Your partner, Richie? The one in your nightmare?"

Angela suddenly remembered the incident at the Hanalei when she had called out for Richie. Her hands grew clammy and she felt weak. "He's been staying here this week."

Chip stopped abruptly. "Are you okay? I mean . . . what was he doing here?"

Angela felt embarrassed to admit her predicament. "He was here. That's all."

"But, Angel?"

Angela looked up and down the street. Although no one

was around, she didn't want an audience. There was no delaying this show-down. "Let's go inside, okay?"

She pushed open the front door, allowed Chip to pass, and closed it behind her. The walls that had been so confining all week seemed unbearably close. Chip settled himself on the couch that Richie had only recently vacated. Her living room still looked occupied, with left-over soda cans, napkins and discarded newspapers scattered across the coffee table.

Angela took a deep breath and sat across from him on a plump leather chair. Chip looked uncomfortable and concerned as he waited for her to speak.

"Want something to drink?" she offered.

"No thanks." He leaned forward, interlocking his fingers and resting his forearms on his knees. "What's this all about?"

Angela struggled with her emotions. Before she could control them, her feelings escaped and exclaimed, "Chip, this is hard for me."

Chip looked shaken, as if anticipating bad news. "Honey, whatever it is, you can talk to me about it. I'm willing to work with you—just tell me what you need."

"I'm so used to being strong, being in control. Right now it seems now I don't have any."

Chip stood and eased around the coffee table that separated them. Gently, he took her hand and coaxed her from her chair. His kindness and strength urged her over the edge of self-control. To her disdain, she sobbed and pressed her face, wet with tears, against his rock-solid chest. "I didn't want you to come."

"I told you I'd be here," he soothed. "I'll always be here for you."

"I didn't want you to know."

"It can't be so bad. Come on now, what's troubling you?"

"I—I've got problems at work."

Chip held her without speaking.

"Richie came to help me."

"I can appreciate that, darlin', but whatever it is, surely you can talk to me about it."

No, she wanted to scream. *I don't want to tell you. I can't admit how foolish I was. How stupid. How inexperienced.* Angela covered her face with her hands.

"Angel?"

She shook her head and lowered her eyes. "I can't, Chip."

"But honey—"

"I don't know if I can complicate my professional life with my personal life right now." A tear escaped and rolled down her face, followed by another. "As much as I wanted to believe I could be happy with you—" Carefully, she slipped the diamond ring from her finger.

"No, honey. Don't."

Angela held the ring between them. "I think we should wait, Chip. Don't make this harder than it already is."

Reluctantly, Chip took the ring and held it between his thumb and forefinger.

"Tell your mother I'm sorry."

"Just like that?" His face held disbelief. "You think I can walk away and forget you?"

"You need to."

"Angel, I love you. We're a team. We're meant for each other. I know it as well as I'm looking at you."

"I don't love you," she lied. *I don't know how. I don't know if I ever will.*

Her words startled him as surely as if he'd been slapped. "That's different then, isn't it?"

She nodded in agreement.

"I suppose I should go." The captain's head lowered and his shoulders bowed in defeat as he slipped the ring into the breast pocket of his uniform jacket.

Don't go, she wanted to shout. *I need you.* But her words remained unspoken. *He should go. He'll be better off without me, I'm sure.*

She swallowed hard and tried to control her quavering voice. "I'll let you out."

As she opened the door for him, a bright light flashed, forcing her back.

A reporter pushed a microphone at her. "Miss Lawrey? I want to ask a few questions."

Chip brushed past her, reacting instantly. Thrusting his arms out, in a protective gesture, he stated, "Miss Lawrey has no comment. Please respect her privacy. She would like you to leave."

The camera flashed again as the photographer hoisted his equipment above Chip's head and took another shot.

Chip grasped the man's arm.

"Whoa, buddy. Are you the boyfriend or what?" the reporter asked.

Angela slammed the door shut, leaving Chip to deal with the local paparazzi. If she thought she had been a prisoner before, this left her no doubt. She watched the men through the window in the door and listened as Chip fielded the reporter's questions.

The newsman was pushy, bordering on rude, but Chip spoke in a calm and calculating manner, and firmly repeated, "Miss Lawrey has no comment. You've been asked to leave. Any further intrusion will be met with the police."

The cameraman took a picture of Chip, then backed away as the pilot glared at him. He demanded to know Chip's name and what their relationship was.

Ignoring his queries, Chip interrupted. "Understandably Miss Lawrey needs time to herself." He pointed to their car. "I won't ask you again."

The disgruntled pair backed off then turned when they were out of the pilot's reach. Chip remained on the porch until they had pulled away and were out of sight.

He let himself back into the house. Behind the door, the newspaper lay on the floor. The headline was bold and blatant. *FEMALE CONTROLLER CITED AS CAUSE.*

Chip picked up the paper and began reading. His face transformed from disappointment to disbelief. "You?"

Angela snatched the paper from his grasp. "Yes, it's me. It's all me!" Sobbing, she flung the paper across the room. "I did it."

"But, honey you can't blame yourself—"

"Oh, Chip," she collapsed against him. "I've ruined everything."

"No, honey. No." It pained him deeply that the woman he loved did not trust him with what mattered most: her feelings. He felt as helpless as the day Rayanne had been injured. He wasn't able to help Rayanne then, anymore than he was able to help Angela now. Filled with a protective fierceness, the Captain grasped Angela's arms and turned her to face him. "Hear me out. This may be the hardest thing you've ever done, but you've got to fight. You're strong. You'll be all right."

Angela broke completely as sobs convulsed her. Chip cradled her head against his shoulder, allowing her to lean against him as she let fall a torrent of previously unspent tears.

"I'll never be able to go back there."

"You will. I'll help you."

"I can't ask you to do that," she argued.

"Who's asking?"

"What about you? Maybe you shouldn't get involved."

"What can they do to me?" The captain smiled. "Honey, I know it's bad, but time will help. Believe me. I know what I'm talking about."

"How do you know?"

"I need to tell you something, Angel." He guided her to her chair. "Please. It's been weighing heavy on me ever since we left the ranch."

"What is it, Chip?" Angela stemmed her tears and listened to the man who's face now reflected pain.

"Honey, I didn't want to tell you—" The pilot breathed deeply. "But I was behind the wheel when Rayanne died. I killed her."

"No." The words tore from her throat before she thought to subdue them. "What do you mean?"

"*I* should have died, not her. For years I blamed myself for Rayanne's death. I lost my wife, Bobby lost his mother, and after it all, I thought I would die. I hate to say it, but I wanted to die."

"But it couldn't have been your fault," she said, disbelieving. "It was an accident, wasn't it?"

"Sure it was. But you couldn't convince me of that at the time. I killed my wife. I should have been more careful. I should have been stronger, smarter, better. I loved her, and because of me she's gone."

"But it wasn't your fault," she argued.

"And it wasn't your fault, either." His face was stern, serious.

"But this is different," she challenged. "There were over two hundred people on that plane."

"You weren't in control of that loss anymore than I was," Chip soothed. "It's tragic. It hurt a lot of people's lives. But, honey, sometimes we human beings cannot control what's beyond our grasp. You are no more to blame than I was. The hard part is surviving the guilt."

Angela nodded in spite of her tears. She understood. It didn't make the pain go away, but she would learn to accept the truth. She was on hand, but not the guiding force that saved or condemned Flight 155.

Chip cleared his throat. "I spent a lot of time trying to drown my grief. Lost some of Bobby's most precious years trying to hide from my guilt and shame. And it's hard for me to admit, but you hit too close to home when you asked me if I was still in love with Rayanne. I don't think I'll ever get over her. She was my first love. We were crazy about each other. I wasted a lot of time chasing her ghost. I looked for her face in every brunette I saw. But it was never her.

"I know it seems crazy but it took me years to accept that she was gone—and to stop dreaming about her. I knew in my heart she was in a better place, but I just couldn't accept it. It's a wonder my whole family didn't give up on me."

"But they didn't," she reminded him.

"And we're not giving up on you, either." The captain stood and held out his hands to her. "I'm not fooling myself, Angela. There's never going to be another Rayanne. And I have fallen in love with you. Not a memory. Not a recreation. No one can come close to you. And now that I've found you—"

Wordlessly, Angela placed her hand in his. She allowed him, once more, to slip the ring onto her finger.

"Angela Lawrey, I love you. I believe you love me and I want to spend my life with you." He paused. "Don't shut me out of your life, honey."

Angela molded herself to him and listened to the steady beating of his heart. They stood in silence until Angela felt her knees weaken.

"I can't explain the resemblance. I guess I have a weakness for a good-looking woman, and I happen to like the way your dark hair contrasts with your pretty skin." He brushed her cheek with the back of his hand. "But I can't help that. Some guys like redheads, some like blonds."

Angela murmured. "I kinda like the way you look too, Captain."

"There. See what I mean?"

Angela smiled. She noted the tired lines around his blue eyes. "You've convinced me," she whispered. "I know it'll take some time, and I've got a lot to do, but I'll work at it."

"We'll be all right," he assured her, then gently kissed her lips. "Listen, I've got to get back to the airport. I'll call you in a few days, okay?"

"I—I need to try to get through this on my own, Chip. If I don't—"

Chip studied her somberly. "You can do it. I know you can. And I'm always here if you need me."

Angela nodded. "Thanks, Chip.

He lifted her fingers to his lips and kissed them. "I'll wait to hear from you."

The latch clicked shut after he left, and Angela locked the door then leaned back against it for support. She was physically and emotionally depleted. Unconsciously, she twisted the delicate ring on her finger and watched as it sparkled in the diffused light. Chip loved her. She knew it. And she would survive this challenge with his love backing her up.

Around noon on Sunday Richie phoned. Just to check on her, he said.

"So how was the good Captain? He didn't look too happy."

"Did you see what they printed in the paper today?" she asked.

"Yeah. Tough break—naming the Captain and all."

Angela pondered his comment. She had heard the reporter ask Chip for his name, but she was certain he hadn't given it. How did they find out who he was?

"They must have come right after I left, huh?"

"Yeah. About ten minutes later. Did you see them?"

"I . . . uh . . . thought I saw someone pulling into your complex. Two guys."

"But how'd they get the code to pass through the electronic gate?"

"Maybe it's not that secure," Richie suggested. "Locks usually keep the honest ones out."

How had they entered? Angela wondered.

She spent the rest of the afternoon cleaning the condo, grateful to have mindless tasks that would keep her from her self-critical thoughts. Hours passed while she busied herself with the household chores. By evening, she allowed herself a break.

When she stopped working, however, the small voices began, gnawing at her conscience like a dog would a bone. Angela resorted to the medication the doctor prescribed to help her sleep. Eventually, she succumbed to sleep and got through one more night.

Getting dressed for work on Monday morning was one of the hardest tasks Angela had faced recently. She knew she would be the object of gossip and speculation. There wasn't a person in Longmont who hadn't read in the local paper that she was the female controller in question. She dressed carefully, knowing that everyone would be watching her. She felt as if she were already on trial.

She made it past the guard and through the gate without any encounter. The real test would be the gauntlet past her peers. She dreaded the looks, and expected pity, disdain, even contempt. What she received was a little of each, depending upon the level of rapport she had developed individually with each controller.

She marched past the control room and reported to the training area where she would be undergoing her refresher course for the next couple of weeks. It was humiliating, but she tried to appear as if it didn't matter. It was just another aspect of her job. Deep inside, however, she was mortified.

At the end of the week, Angela garnered her courage to call Chip. She dialed the number to his Los Angeles home. She waited through three rings, then heard the mechanical message, "The number you have reached—" Angela couldn't believe it. She dialed the number again. When the same message began playing, she replaced the handset on the receiver as if it carried a virus. *It couldn't be. Where was he*? With trepidation, she dialed the number to the Stephens' ranch.

The phone rang twice. Each ring tore at a place deep within her.

"Hello?" a man's voice boomed.

"Pops?"

"Angel? Is that you?"

"Yes. It's Angela."

"How are you, girl?"

She drew a deep breath. "Not so good."

"What's the matter?"

"Have you—have you seen Robert?"

"Yes. He flew in Saturday night. He was about as distracted as a tumbleweed in a tornado."

Her stomach knotted and she felt an uncomfortable heat rush upward. She knew, without looking, that her face blazed.

"I—uh—did he say anything? I mean, do you know how I can reach him?"

"Said something about movin' out of that apartment of his. Said it was past due for a change."

Angela felt lead in the spot her stomach used to be. Perhaps he had given up on her, after all.

"Anything I can do?" the older man offered.

"I just needed to talk to someone."

"Well, I'm not as good-looking as that boy o' mine, but you don't have to look at me over the phone."

"You're sweet, Pops. I'll just—" her courage waned and Angela heard her voice crack. "Oh, Pops. I do need to speak with you—I don't know who else to turn to. Chip may have given up on me."

"Now don't shut the gate just yet, Angel."

Angela squeezed her eyes shut, vainly trying to stay her tears. "I'll just call back—"

"Now hold on, Angel. We're going to talk, but first I want you to listen. Are you with me now?"

"Yes."

"I know what happened out there, but I'm telling you there ain't nothin' so bad that you can't get over it."

"But," she whimpered. "They all died."

"I know, honey. I know."

"He told you?"

"He did."

"I guess everyone knows by now." She felt her throat go dry. "I felt so useless, Pops. I didn't know what to do. I couldn't help them."

"No one could, Angel. Not you, not the pilots, not the whole dang world."

"But, Pops, you don't understand."

"There's a lot I don't understand, but I'm simple enough not to question the Lord's doing. We don't know, and have no right to question His design."

Pops' words quieted Angela. All the hours she had spent with the therapist had not eased her conscience as Pops had.

"Now you listen to me, Angel. I know what kind of salt you're made of. You've got grit and intelligence and courage. Are you listening?"

"Yes, sir."

"Don't you let those slick-tongued lawyers talk you into admittin' anything. You couldn't control the weather. You weren't behind the reins. All you could do was try to guide that plane out of danger, but there wasn't a place high enough or far enough or safe enough. Lord knows you did all you could in your power to save them, but it wasn't in your hands. Isn't that right?"

"Yes, sir. That's right."

"Then I don't want you blamin' yourself for something that couldn't be helped. You done all you could and that's all there is to it."

"Thank you, Pops. I'm grateful to you."

"Is there going to be a trial or something?"

"They're conducting an investigation right now. If FAA

believes it wasn't my fault then they'll defend me against a national inquiry."

"Do you want me to come out there and stand by you?"

"No, Pops. You don't need to do that. If there's a trial it'll be a long time from now. I'll be all right." *If they find me innocent.*

"I know you will. You're a strong woman. You'll come out the best on this, mark my words."

"You think so?"

"Honey, I know it as well as I know myself. Some things in life are designed to temper us, like forgin' horseshoes in the fire. It's gonna be tough, but it'll make you tougher."

Angela felt a measure of strength, deep within her, struggling to surface. She knew that Pops was right. She could and she would get through this. She felt determined, now, to try.

"Thank you for helping me, Pops. Have you heard from Rob this week?"

"No, but I expect him to be calling, though," Pops continued. "Do you want me to tell him—"

"No. But thank you. You've been a big help."

"We're here if you need us, honey. You hear?"

"Yes. I just wish my life wasn't so extreme. It seems like it's either really high or really low. I wish it could be more in the middle of the road."

"Darlin', there ain't nothin' in the middle of the road but yellow stripes and dead armadillos, and neither one suits you."

On Friday, after Angela had completed the last battery of tests for her refresher course, she and Richie were on their way to the break room. Sam Rankin intercepted them in the hallway.

"Haskell wants to see you," Rankin informed her. "Ten o'clock Monday." He turned and walked away without further conversation.

"About as warm as an iceberg in the Arctic." Richie mused. "So, you're either condemned or redeemed. Which is it?"

"I wonder," Angela responded. "Couldn't they bother to give me a hint?"

"And spoil your weekend? This way you can fret about it for two whole days. With any luck you might get some sleep before you show up Monday."

"You're such a pessimist, Rich."

"A pessimist is a realist who isn't disappointed," Richie instructed. "You, on the other hand, are an optimist who is always disappointed. Am I right?"

Angela cocked her head thoughtfully. "I'll take your word for it."

"So rest easy this weekend. I'm going to," he assured her.

"Thanks."

Chapter Eleven

"Y̲ou're in luck, Lawrey. The Center's recordings cleared you of any wrongdoing. Now it's up to the airline manufacturer and FAA to determine whose fault it was. As far as we're concerned, you've been reinstated." Haskell peered at her over the top of his half-rimmed glasses.

"You mean I'm—"

"You've been reassigned—back to your station."

"So when can I go back to work?"

"Tomorrow."

Angela looked toward the ceiling and breathed in deeply. The past few weeks proved the toughest she had endured in her entire life. If Pops was to be believed, she had emerged—tested, tougher, stronger. And she had won. She settled her gaze on her supervisor.

"Bob?"

"Yes."

"Tell me the truth. Was there anything I could have done?"

He shook his head sadly. "Nothing. It was a freak wind. It could have happened to anyone."

Why me?, she wondered. She stood and reached across the desk to shake Bob's hand. "Thank you, Bob."

"Don't thank me. You did your job, I did mine."

"Where do we go from here?"

"What do you mean?"

Angela breathed in deeply. "The rumors, the gossip— will there be a formal announcement?"

"Just do your job, Lawrey. I don't think we need to belabor the point. A formal statement will be issued to the media—"

"By whom?"

"The Center Director—through the proper channels, of course."

"So I won't need to worry about being hounded at my front door?"

Haskell shook his head. "I still don't understand that. Your name was never released. It had to have come from inside."

Angela pondered Haskell's comment. But from *who*?

"Whoever it is," Haskell warned, "we're still looking for him."

"Or her," Angela added.

"We have our suspicions, but until we have hard evidence, we have nothing."

Bob dismissed her when the phone rang at his desk. "We'll talk again soon," he promised.

Angela let herself out of his office. Closing the door behind her, she could no longer restrain her relief. Emotionally, she felt ten pounds lighter. Fully cleared to return to work, and she was more than ready.

* * *

The next morning, the young controller reported to her station. It seemed she had been gone much longer than the three weeks since the accident. A nagging nervousness settled in her stomach as she donned her headset and tuned into the area frequency. In seconds, she would be on line.

Richie sauntered close to Angela's side and feigned a golfing stance. Holding his invisible club, he drew back and swung, following through with his entire body. He cupped his right hand above his brow as if watching the invisible ball until it landed. "Hole in one," he shouted. "Did you see that?"

His playfulness was infectious, and Angela found herself laughing at his antic.

"You'll never grow up, Richie," she teased.

"I'll find some good looking babe who makes lots of money one of these days," Richie vowed. "Then I can blow this popsicle stand."

Angela eyed him wryly.

"In the meantime, I'll work on my game," he announced, feigning another shot at a golf ball.

"Play time's over, Lange." Sam Rankin chided. "Back to work." He nodded curtly at Angela, acknowledging her presence.

Richie glared at him as he passed.

Angela, sensing her partner's mood shift, patted his hand. "Leave it alone, Richie."

"Who died and made him king?" Richie retorted.

"Come on. Let's get to work." Angela urged Richie to take his place beside her at the data position seat.

"Sure, Ang. Whatever you say," he snapped.

Angela had noticed a difference in Richie since he had left her apartment. It could have been her imagination, but her partner seemed agitated and moody—unlike his normal carefree façade.

But Angela had her own worries. Following her forced refresher, she maintained a guarded approach to her work, her words and her actions. She didn't dare risk further embarrassment to herself or the Center with any mistakes—personal or professional.

She missed Chip. In spite of herself, she worried that perhaps he had finally come to his senses and realized what she had previously feared: they didn't belong together.

The following weekend, she boarded the plane that would take her to San Antonio. The Stephens didn't know she was coming and that's the way Angela wanted it. She rented a car at the airport and followed the same route that Chip had driven her a month ago. It seemed as if a year had passed. The spring rain swelled the little river as Angela wound through the hills and made her way to the Stephens' ranch.

It was mid-afternoon when she stepped from the car. She was met by Jasper, barking and bounding toward her. The front door opened and Angela was greeted by a stern-faced teen.

"Bobby Ray?"

"Hi. What are you doing here? Where's dad?"

Angela mounted the steps to the Stephens' home. "I don't know. I saw him last week, briefly."

Jasper pawed at her feet and whimpered, eagerly vying for attention.

"Down, Jas," Bobby Ray scolded. "Stay down."

The dog hunkered down, head between its paws, raising its eyes expectantly.

"He's okay," Angela bent down and scratched the dog's head. "Jasper and I are friends, aren't we, boy?"

"What do you mean, last week? I thought you two—"

Angela leveled her gaze at the young man. Her study

revealed a chin as strong and proud as his father's, eyes the same blue as his grandmother's, and a young man's face full of questions.

She shook her head. "I've been tied up at work and your father's been busy himself, I'm sure."

Bobby Ray looked confused.

"I came to speak to Dorothy and Pops. Are they here?"

Bobby Ray lowered his head and kicked uncomfortably at an invisible target. "They're in Houston. Pops is looking at a piece of farming equipment."

"And you didn't go with him?"

"I'm studying for finals. You wanna come in?" Awkwardly, he held the screen door open.

Angela shrugged. "Sure. I'll stay a little while."

Bobby Ray led her inside. Textbooks covered the dining room table. Country music played low on the living room stereo. His cowboy boots rested by the front door. The young man was not as tall as Chip. His white T-shirt tucked into his jeans revealed a muscular frame similar to his father's. Angela again felt a tug of regret pulling on her heart.

"Want some coffee?" he offered.

"Yes. That would be nice."

She seated herself at the far end of the table. Bobby Ray brought a cup of coffee that looked so black and thick, it must have sat on the burner all day. The opened textbooks revealed a trigonometry lesson that seemed to be troubling him, if the sheets of crumpled paper were an indication.

Angela sipped the strong brew, but held it in her mouth before swallowing. It tasted as if it were the morning coffee that had, indeed, cooked all day.

"Is it okay?" Bobby Ray asked. "I don't drink the stuff myself."

Angela set the cup down. "It's all right." Eyeing his books, she said "How's the studying coming along?"

"Trig is tough." He closed the book. "I'm having a hard time with it."

"Mind if I take a look?"

"Go ahead." He shoved the book in her direction. "I'm stuck."

She read through the question and flipped back to the beginning of the chapter. She was aware of Bobby Ray watching her as she moved her finger over the text, speed-reading the information.

"Wow. Are you some kind of genius or something?"

"No." Angela continued her fast-scanning until she reached the point where he had quit. "I think I've got it. Do you want me to go over it with you?"

"Sure."

Bobby Ray pulled up a chair and bent over the text as she explained the formula. She was pleased that he seemed to grasp her explanation. Some time later, she looked at her watch and discovered forty five minutes had passed.

"I didn't intend to stay this long, Bobby Ray."

"No. It's—all right," he stammered. "I'm glad you did."

"I came to tell your folks that I wouldn't be here for your graduation as I had promised."

"Oh?" He appeared disappointed. "Was that because of me?"

"No, not at all," she soothed. "Actually, it was my doing. I'm afraid I've spoiled things."

"How? How could you? I mean—"

Angela listened as the music switched from a light-hearted country tune to a soulful female singer lamenting a lost love. She felt like the fool the singer described in her country song.

She drew a large white envelope from her purse and handed it to Chip's son. "I had promised Pops I'd come, but I—I can't be here that weekend. I brought this for you."

Bobby Ray took the envelope and frowned. "You know I probably shouldn't have—"

"It's okay, Bobby Ray. I'm glad I saw the picture. I feel for your loss. I hope you know that."

The young man nodded. "I never thought about the way dad must have felt. He's entitled to a bit of happiness himself. It's not like I'll be your son or anything."

Angela dropped her gaze. *It would never be like he was her son. Not now, not ever. My loss, Bobby Ray*, she thought.

"Listen, I'd better go. Tell Dorothy—I mean your grandmother and Pops—that I stopped by."

"You flew in just to say hello?" The teen looked astounded.

"I wanted to keep my word, Bobby Ray."

"You can't stay?"

"Nah. I better get going. I made reservations in San Antonio. I'll fly out in the morning."

"You've got time for a ride then?"

"What?"

"Paint. Don't you want to take a ride?"

Angela started to decline, but sensed an underlying plea in his voice.

"Pops said you liked Paint."

"I did. I mean—I do."

"Well then?"

She looked down at her silk slacks and sandaled feet.

"I'll get you some clothes."

"What about your studies?"

"You got me through the hard part. I can finish the rest later."

"Bobby Ray, are you sure?"

The teenager acted as excited as Chip when he was happy. For an instant the smile was the same as his father's. He slipped into his boots and shouted, "I'll be right back," as he bolted out the back door. Within minutes he returned with a pair of his jeans, a T-shirt, extra boots and his grandmother's cowboy hat. "I'll bet these'll fit you," he stated, dumping the pile at her feet.

"I'll go saddle the horses."

Before she could even think about protesting, Bobby Ray left as quickly as he came. She ducked into the bathroom and changed. As he had guessed, his extra clothes fit well enough.

She sauntered out to the corral about the time Bobby Ray finished cinching the saddle on the lively mare. The little paint eyed the newcomer, twitching its ears back and forth.

"Hey, girl," Angela patted the paint's neck. "Remember me?"

"Sure she does. She's a smart little mare." Bobby Ray swung his leg high and mounted Pops' big bay mare. "Ready?"

Angela slipped her foot into the stirrup, mounted up and nodded.

"Let's ride."

Bobby Ray clucked and both horses moved forward, seeming anxious to get out. The two cantered side by side until the ranch house was just a speck in the distance. It was warmer than the first time she rode over the Stephens' ranch. She felt the sun on her arms and lifted her face to the Texas sky.

"You okay?" the young man asked.

"Uh-huh."

"Feels good, huh?"

"It does. Thanks, Bobby Ray."

The young cowboy nodded.

They rode quite a while in silence until Bobby Ray spoke up. "Dad said you had some trouble last month."

It shouldn't have surprised her that the incident had been discussed in front of Bobby Ray. It *had* made the national news, after all. She couldn't help feeling that same leaden weight settle in her stomach.

She nodded. "It wasn't fun."

"Yes'm."

"I never thought I would be involved in an accident like that. You always think that happens to someone else."

The boy nodded. His young face bore the knowledge of someone who had experienced loss early on.

"You know what I mean."

"I think I do. I'm sure my parents never dreamed it would go the way it did for them."

"I lost my mother, too, Bobby Ray. Not like you did. But sometimes I think it was just as bad. You see, I haven't spoken to her since I was fourteen. She left home and left me. She had a choice—your mother didn't."

"That doesn't seem right," the boy answered. "I mean, she's your *mother*."

"Well, I had my dad. He didn't talk much and I don't think he ever said he loved me, but I think he does. In his own way."

"That makes it hard, I'd think," the young man admitted. "I blamed my dad a lot for not being around, but he had to fly. That's what he does."

"It's hard when you're a kid to understand that, Bobby Ray. You've had to grow up early."

"We did all right. I love this ranch. This land. I wouldn't have wanted it any other way."

"We better get back, don't you think?" Angela tugged the reins to the right, urging the mare toward the corral.

"I'm glad you rode with me, Miss—Angela."

Angela chuckled. "You're about as persuasive as your father, Bobby Ray. It was my pleasure."

Angela helped Bobby Ray wipe down the horses, curry them, and turn them into the corral. He followed her inside the house. When she emerged showered, changed and ready to leave, Bobby Ray met her in the dining room. His expression was a mixture of surprise and disbelief.

"A thousand dollars?" He held the opened envelope in his hand. "Miss Lawrey, are you sure about this?"

Angela smiled, remembering how she had acquired that money. "It was a gift, Bobby Ray. I'm just passing it along."

"But that's a lot of money, and you're not even—"

"Family," she added. "I know."

"I don't mean any disrespect, ma'am."

"It's okay, Bobby Ray. It's just a down payment on your education. It'll take a lot more than that to see you through." She patted his shoulder. "Do yourself proud, okay?"

"Yes, ma'am."

Angela let herself out the front door and got into the car. Bobby Ray waved as she pulled out of the drive under the bright blue Texas sky.

Chapter Twelve

The following Monday brought yet another challenge. When she arrived at her station she was told to report to Haskell. *Now what,* she thought.

Haskell sat behind his desk, absorbed in a report that lay open before him. He glanced up as she entered, then returned his attention to the papers.

"Morning, Lawrey. Have a seat."

Angela sat stiffly erect.

"Seems like there's a discrepancy in your records. I thought you attended the advanced level aeronautics course at the Academy in Oklahoma City?"

"I did."

"Not according to this, you didn't." Haskell flipped the paperwork upside down so it faced her.

Angela studied the entries, and her eyes widened as she realized that her records had been seamlessly, meticulously, erroneously altered. She clutched the paperwork and looked closer. It appeared as if her background did not include the necessary coursework that qualified her for the position she held.

"What is this? Where did these come from?"

"That's what I'm wondering. I've ordered a duplicate transcript from the ACA."

"How did you happen to find this?" Angela demanded. "What's going on here?"

"Well, during the investigation your background came into question and this paperwork surfaced. I didn't think it was right. As I recall, you came in top of your class—more than qualified. If I didn't know better, I'd say someone was cooking your records."

"But why?" Angela sputtered. "I've done nothing wrong. Why me?"

Haskell's bushy brows raised and he shook his head. "There's some serious sabotage afoot, and unfortunately it appears that you've become a target."

Angela slumped in the chair. "I haven't made any enemies I'm aware of. I can't believe that jealousy would push someone to the point of criminal activity. That's a federal offense, isn't it?

"Yes, it is." Haskell tilted his chair back. "I wouldn't put it past them, whoever they are. I want to caution you, Lawrey . . . keep this to yourself."

"Who would I tell?"

"I'm saying, don't talk to anyone. Not your parents, not your working partner, not your boyfriend—no one."

Angela felt her face color. "I'm not in the habit—"

"Don't get upset, Lawrey. I'm just saying that what you saw here can't leave this room. I had to check it out with you, but I don't want *anyone* to know we're onto them."

"This is not the cold war, you know."

"It is as far as I'm concerned. I need your cooperation."

"Are you going to set a trap?"

"It's in the works," he admitted. "Altering federal documents is a felony. We are not treating this as a prank."

Angela shivered in response to Haskell's directive. He was serious—this had gone beyond a level of toleration. What concerned her was the degree of harm someone intended. *Was she that threatening? What if they resorted to personal attack when all else failed?* It frightened her to think about it.

"Have I got your word you'll cooperate?" Haskell repeated.

"Of course."

"Good. Now get back to work."

Angela pulled herself from the chair and started to leave the office. "I'm calling others in, Lawrey. I don't want it to appear you've been singled out. Understand?"

Angela nodded. She pulled the door to his office closed behind her.

Richie had taken two weeks of personal leave, so Angela worked with another partner while he was off. She worked well with others, but missed that special rapport she had cultivated with Richie. The week was uneventful, following the discussion with Haskell on Monday.

Chip had left a message on her answering machine, thanking her for the gift she had given Bobby Ray. At least she had done something right for the Stephens clan. They had been more than kind to her.

A certified copy of her transcript arrived by courier a few days later. It was as Angela had said, and as Haskell believed. Someone had painstakingly recreated her records and understated her qualifications. This person had done a flawless job but, if caught, would face prosecution.

The noose was tightening. Angela suspected, and Haskell confirmed, that FBI agents, posing as air conditioning contractors, were brought in to launch their own investigation. They were setting up secret surveillance equipment. Hidden cameras were installed and bugging devices put in place.

When Richie returned the following Monday, the Center was typically somber and low-key. It seemed nothing had changed. Richie, on the other hand, had acquired a tan and was looking a little less gloomy than when he had left.

"That two weeks at the Tucson golf school must have done you good, Richie. You're in much better spirits than when you left."

"Yep." He patted the brightly colored island-motif shirt, and preened, puffing out his chest. "Had a bevy of women around me the whole time. Couldn't keep 'em off me."

"Not one of them under sixty," a controller teased.

"Hey—this is my story," Richie countered. "Let me tell it."

Angela giggled. "Did you find a rich babe?"

"Close. I made a few friends."

"Good for you, Richie. I'm glad you had a break. You needed it."

"What do you mean?" he challenged. His tone was harsh, and he seemed threatened.

"Nothing. I just meant I'm glad you had some time off, that's all."

Richie's face mellowed almost instantly. "Oh. Yeah. Well, we've all been under a strain lately."

"I know." Angela watched her partner closely. He had seriously overreacted to her innocent comment. His behavior was obvious to everyone. It worried her. Perhaps the stress had been too much for him. She considered talking to him about seeking counseling, but decided against it. She would, however, bring it up to Haskell when they spoke again.

By the fourth day, the FBI intervention had apparently paid off. Word circulated inside the building in a matter of hours. It seemed that everyone had been alerted to the fact that someone's image had been captured in the records room. The culprit had not been named, and the victim not yet identified, but the Feds had their man.

Late in the afternoon, following her shift, Sam Rankin approached Angela.

"Haskell wants to see you."

Angela wanted to shake some emotion onto his dead-pan face. Richie was right about him—he was as readable as a poker player.

"He's got some bad news, Lawrey."

"Tell me something I don't know. Anytime I get called in to his office it's bad news." Wordlessly she followed him into the dark corridor that led to Haskell's office.

Suddenly Angela caught a glimpse of Richie, flanked by two uniformed officers. She gasped, involuntarily, when she saw his hands cuffed behind his back. Richie must have sensed her presence if he hadn't heard her voice. Turning, he looked at her and grinned.

"Say, Ang. No hard feelings, huh?"

"Richie?" She stared at him in disbelief. "What's going on?"

He shrugged, his same boyish self she was accustomed to.

"Doesn't matter now, does it?"

"You?"

"So? I didn't have a leg up like you did. Funny thing— you don't belong here, and you get to stay. Crazy, huh?"

Angela stood rigid, shocked.

"Go back to your Nebraska farm, Ang. Or, better yet, hook up with your flyboy. He'll make enough for both of you."

The officer tugged at Richie's arm, forcing him forward.

"I've worked for everything I've gotten, Richie. Nobody gave it to me."

"Let it go, Lawrey," Sam urged. "He's not himself. You know that."

"But—what's wrong? What did I do?"

"It's not you. He's got more problems than he ever let on here."

Sam pushed open the door to Haskell's office. He waited to enter until Angela stepped inside, then stood beside her.

"You'd better sit down," Haskell suggested.

Angela sighed wearily and folded herself into the chair.

"They've picked up Lange," Haskell announced solemnly.

"We met them in the hall," Rankin explained.

"Who? The Feds?"

Sam nodded.

Haskell rolled his eyes. "I asked them to use discretion."

If Haskell hadn't looked so serious, Angela would have laughed. It had to be a joke. "You're kidding, right? This is a joke, isn't it?"

Haskell looked at her as if she had lost her mind. "I don't think you understand, Lawrey. They caught him on tape. He admitted he falsified your records—that and a lot more."

Angela felt the color drain from her face, and she felt light-headed. She clutched the arms of the chair. "I don't believe it. Not Richie."

"We've been monitoring him for some time, but we had no idea he was capable of criminal behavior."

"What do you mean?"

"His medical condition."

"What medical condition?"

"Bipolar disorder. Manic depressive."

"Richie?" Angela shook her head, searching her memory for signs even she had overlooked.

"He's been seeing a therapist, but it seems like the medication was too little, too late."

"When?"

"The two weeks he took off—"

"He was playing golf," she interrupted.

"He was institutionalized," Sam corrected. "He tried to keep it confidential but the medical officer was alerted."

Angela tried to stand, but didn't trust her legs to hold her. She slumped back into the chair. Tears blinded her eyes and she felt her throat tighten. She couldn't speak.

"I'm sorry," Haskell soothed. "I know it's a shock."

"I thought he was just kidding around, but he did seem to become more agitated these past couple of months."

"Take a couple of days, Lawrey. I'll write it off as comptime."

Angela stood and breathed deeply. "What next?"

"You going to be all right?"

"Yes." She turned to leave. "I'm going home."

"Walk her out, will you, Sam?"

Sam opened the door for her and waited as she gathered her purse and jacket. When they reached the outer door, he shoved his hands into his pockets and shifted his gaze to the floor.

"Sorry about Richie, Lawrey."

"Me too, Sam. It's hard to believe. I always thought—"

"I know. You thought I was out to get your job, didn't you?"

Angela felt her face coloring. She didn't deny what Sam believed to be true.

"I know it must have appeared that way at times." He shuffled his feet. "I've been pretty hard on you."

"It doesn't matter."

Sam sighed. "We've all been under an inordinate amount of stress. Richie just finally snapped."

"He was my friend. I can't believe I didn't know."

Sam draped his arm around her shoulder. "Don't blame yourself," he whispered. "It's not your fault."

She allowed Sam to walk her to her car.

"They'll get him the help he needs?"

Sam nodded.

"They won't put him in jail, will they?"

"Hard telling. I suspect he'll be medically discharged."

Angela covered her mouth with a trembling hand. "Oh, Richie," she whispered. She turned to face Sam. "I wish there was something I could have done."

"You're his friend. He's still going to need that." Sam gave her a brotherly squeeze. "You'll be okay?"

She nodded and wiped a tear. Thrusting her chin upward, she took a deep breath, straightened her shoulders and exhaled. "I'll see you Monday." She unlocked her car, eased in and fitted the key into the ignition. Angela felt a fierce urge to break free. She had been so wrong about everyone . . . Sam, Richie, Chip, even herself. As she started the engine and allowed it to idle, she picked up her mobile phone and dialed.

"Pops, it's Angela."

"Angel? How are you doin', girl?"

"On a scale of one to ten? I'd have to say a two."

"Well now, that's a little bit higher than a snake's belly. Things must be looking up."

"I have to reach Chip. Do you know where he is?"

"Well," Pops drawled. "I suspect he's workin' on that house of his."

"Has he got a phone?"

"Don't think so."

Angela didn't hesitate. "Pops I've got to go. I'm going to find him."

"Wait a minute! He said we could reach him on his cellular."

She dialed in the number Pops had given her and waited. His voice mail answered, but Angela elected not to leave a message.

Dejectedly, she pulled into her garage, closed the door and walked into her condominium. A ringing phone met her as she entered. She threw her purse and keys onto the counter and snatched the handset from the receiver.

"Hello."

"Angel?"

"Chip, I need to see you! I've missed you."

He sighed audibly. "That's what I was hopin' for. Honey, I haven't been able to walk and talk proper since I saw you last.

"Me either," she admitted.

"Let me see you. I'm in town—"

"Denver?"

"Outside of Longmont, actually."

"Longmont? What are you doing here?"

"On my way to see you."

"Really?" She felt as excited as a teen expecting a date. "I'll be there in a few minutes."

A short time later he arrived, dressed in a casual knit shirt paired with cowboy boots and jeans.

"Come on," he coaxed. "I want to show you something."

"Right now?"

"Yep."

"Should I change?"

He grabbed her hand and led her to his car. "Nope."

"Where are we going?"

"For a drive." Gently he slid his hand beneath hers and lifted her fingers to his lips. "It's good to see you."

Angela wouldn't admit to herself that her days had seemed void of life without him. Now, beside Chip, she at least felt able to breathe.

As they drove out of town, he urged the vehicle around a right-turning curve. Chip shifted into second and began the winding climb up the North Saint Vrain canyon. The late afternoon sun was low.

"Pops said they cleared you. Is that final?"

"When did you—?"

"Just talked to him."

"That's why I got your voice mail," she mused.

"I was checking in and he said you'd just called."

"Telepathy," she stated. "I was trying to reach you."

"So what's going on at the Center?"

"They picked up Richie."

"For what?"

"Altering federal documents. Mine, mostly."

Chip clucked his tongue. "Now ain't that enough to make you want to walk in the river 'til your hat floats?"

Angela cocked her head and stared at Chip, not believing what she had heard.

"I learned it from Pops," he chuckled.

Angela started giggling, and Chip responded in kind until the two of them laughed aloud.

"Honey, you'll have to get used to me. I'm afraid I'll never make it as a city boy."

"What have you been doing, Chip? Is it true you've moved?"

"Yes. I have."

"New roommate?"

"Not yet," he answered slowly. "I sure love this drive."

"I didn't bring a jacket. Are we going to Estes?" she asked.

"Not quite."

"You're being awfully mysterious. Where are we going?"

"Just a little further."

The creek alongside the road had grown from a lazy trickle of ice melt to a full-running stream, splashing high on the confining banks. The creekside cottonwood and willow trees were in full foliage, and the brushy growth on both sides of the canyon bloomed brightly with Colorado's weeds and wildflowers. It was all just a blur of color to Angela as they drove through the twisting curves, past the red cliffs that became ribbons of yellow Dakota sandstone.

The warm canyon wind blew past her face, pulling her hair loose from the ponytail she wore. Fine feathery strands tickled her skin and face and she smoothed them back unconsciously.

"So, where did you move?"

Captain Stephens swung the sport utility vehicle off the highway onto a newly excavated dirt road. "Right here," he announced.

Angela's eyes widened as she faced a three-story mountain mansion in the process of being built. The large log home was fully framed. On the second level, a massive redwood deck encircled a south-facing wall of windows.

"My goodness! Are you serious?"

He grinned broadly, obviously pleased with her reaction.

"Yep. You like it?" He bounded from the driver's seat and opened the passenger door for her. "Come on. I want you to see this."

Angela took the hand he offered and together they walked up the sturdy outdoor stairway. When they reached the deck, Angela peered all around. Chip had chosen a perfect location. The house was nestled against the rocks on the north, fully exposed to the east and south. From this vantage point, one could see the Saint Vrain Valley, Boulder, and its surrounding communities. Pine trees and lichen-covered rock dotted the property.

"What do you think?" Chip wrapped his arms around her from behind and gently pulled her close to his chest. "It's a great view, isn't it?"

"It's beautiful, Chip!

"I told you I wanted our own home before we were married—"

"This is your new home?"

"*Our* new home."

As she entered, she heard music playing softly. Angela peered up to the loft above the expansive log-beamed living room. The walls were layered like Lincoln logs, slotted into each other. Skylights opened the room with airiness, bathing the spacious room in light.

The kitchen opened into a combination den and dining room. Chip had installed a granite-topped island that housed an expensive grill and stove top. Double ovens stood beside cabinets and a built-in refrigerator. It was a decorator's dream.

Angela reached for him as if he were a lifeline and burrowed her head into his shoulder.

"What is it, honey? What's the matter?"

"Are you sure you can love me?"

Chip encircled her is his embrace. "After all this time you mean to tell me I haven't convinced you I'm sincere? Honey, I'm hooked as bad as one of those rainbow trout I've been trying to catch. I'm not going anywhere."

"I've been so wrapped up with my own problems I couldn't even see beyond that building. Let me try again, will you?"

Chip hugged her and swayed her gently in his embrace. With a softness she had only dreamed before, he loosened the clip that held her hair in place. The thick, dark mane tumbled onto her shoulders, and Chip gently combed his fingers through it. It seemed the world had disappeared and Angela was aware of nothing but her beating heart and the loving gaze of the man who stood before her. The low music she had heard became clearer, and she recognized the hokey fifties tune that Chip had sung to her when they first danced.

"Want to dance?" Chip whispered.

Angela circled her hands behind his neck and allowed him to lead as they moved to the music.

"Earth angel, earth angel," he crooned. *"Will you be mine?"*

Angela met his loving gaze with one of her own. "You bet I will."